Straw Hat

Lisa-Lin Burke

Straw Hat

COVER DESIGN BY
Jeremy Abbott
www.jabbott.net

Library of Congress
Catalog Card Number: 98-093645

ISBN: 1-57579-135-8

Printed in the United States of America

 PINE HILL PRESS, INC.

Freeman, S. Dak. 57029

For my parents, Donald and Pearl Nichols Burke,
and my mother, Frances Marie Scott Burke.
If not for their love—I would not have been blessed
with this life.

My love-always.

Delia ~ when I got rich &
famous, I'll always remember
our Powder Room Chats!! I've
enjoyed getting to know you
& have appreciated your
support!!

xxx. Jin
10/98

Acknowledgments

These written words could not have become STRAW HAT without the help of some very special people. I owe them more than my gratitude, for they helped my dream become reality.

Kelli Bryant, Donna Huber, Judy Rutledge, and Dewanna Slovak read STRAW HAT in its various stages. Kelli, Donna, and Judy read the very first pages as they rolled off the printer, while Dewanna read the story in its final phase. The four of you presented me with suggestions that made the story what it is today. Thank you.

Jeremy Abbott wore several caps through this never straight as an arrow endeavor. Jeremy, you designed my book's cover, along with the website, and then became an advisor on just about everything. You *challenged* me to make STRAW HAT happen! And somewhere along the way, you became my friend. Thank you.

Valoree McPhillen was my only 'employee', and a non paid one at that! Val read, edited, and gave me constructive criticisms on STRAW HAT. Val, you have never laughed at my dreams! There were times I permitted winds of self-doubt to knock me down, yet you helped me up, brushed me off, and instructed me 'to get over it!' That's what true friends, especially those of three decades, are for. Thank you.

And last but certainly not least, I am beholden to Jim Guinn. Jim, through the years, your support and encouragement never dimmed. You informed me that you knew I was 'passionate about writing.' For that reason alone, you took this risk on my work. Because of you—STRAW HAT is physically here. Because of you—I have learned to fly. Thank you.

Look at a rose—celebrate its beauty.
The rose's scent is
her gift of life to you.

L.L.M.B.

A gentle north wind pushed its way across the Des Moines river, and then against her face. Moon beams danced on the river's peaks. The calendar said it was October, but she swore the scent of roses danced among the north wind's breath. She swallowed the autumn air and smiled.

Resting her elbows on the concrete bridge, bitter exhaust, from a passing car scraped the inside of her nose. The car then belatedly honked. Why bother to acknowledge it?

The lights on Grand Avenue illuminated some of downtown Des Moines. How majestic it looked! A far cry from her girlhood, when she and her sisters traveled from the South Side, to catch a movie, or to spend money they had diligently saved.

Sure, they were poor little colored girls, but they hopped that Metro bus, pretending it to be the biggest and grandest limousine. It brought them to downtown, so they could choose their wares at Kresge's 5 and 10. Sometimes, when they got brave, they'd venture into the most expensive department store, Younkers, just to walk through the cosmetic area.

One day, she knew she'd wear all that pretty stuff. Yes, one day, when she was a registered nurse, she'd have her big house in the best part of Des Moines. Yessiree, that's what she'd have.

She smiled again, and tossed a small stone into the river. Ahh, that was so long ago. Her older sister Mae died a few years ago, and her baby sister, Rose was still here in Des Moines, but she'd not seen her in years. Would Rose even recognize her? If there was time—

"Ma'am? Ma'am?"

"Huh? What?" She turned her head and faced a policeman, evidently walking his beat. He looked as if he were in his twenties. "I beg your pardon, Officer?"

"I'm sorry to bother you, ma'am. Except I've seen you standing here for the past hour or so. And it's getting late. It's nearly midnight."

"Oh," she smiled, "I've been reminiscing. Nothing to be concerned about, I assure you."

"Reminiscing? Nonetheless ma'am, it is pretty late!"

"OK, Officer, Officer—" she squinted to read his nameplate by moonlight. "Officer Iston I just haven't been here in a long time. Des Moines is my hometown."

She watched him smile. "Your hometown?"

"Yes, born and raised. Graduated from East High, a lifetime ago."

"Ahh, really? My mom graduated from East, too! What year did you get out?"

For an officer of the law, he was quite nosy. He should be taking on real criminals. "Oh, let's see, it was 1947 I think. A life time ago."

Laughter erupted from Officer Iston. "Beg your pardon, ma'am, if you were out of East in 1947, you'd be as old as my grandmother, and that can't be! You look about the same age as my mom!"

She gulped hard, her cheeks flushed. "Hey, can't pull anything over one of Des Moines' finest! I was just testing you!" She prayed she recovered.

"You've done a good job. Maybe you knew my mom. She got out in '69 and I popped out in '71. In September, right over there at Lutheran Hospital."

She watched Officer Iston point his club to the northeast, the direction of the hospital. The lump in her throat grew large. Officer Iston was born in September 1971, at Lutheran Hospital. The same hospital, month and year, she—

"My mom's maiden name was Strother? Ring a bell?" He looked at her so anxiously.

Officer Iston's voice snapped her to the present. "Uh, no baby, it doesn't. I got out, uh," she tried to calculate the years in her head. "I graduated in '73, so your mom was gone even before I was a freshman." She hoped he bought the whole story.

"Oh, ok." Officer Iston sounded disappointed. He crossed his arms and never letting his inspection of her cease. "So you've been away."

"Been away?"

"Yes, ma'am, you said you hadn't been back in Des Moines for awhile."

"You're right. Just standing here, it doesn't seem like it's been more than twenty-five years."

"Ah, you left pretty much after graduation then?"

"Uh, yes, you could say that." She wished Officer Iston would go on his way.

"Ma'am, it is close to midnight, and I would feel safer if you were on your way."

"But I'm fine, Officer, truly." She watched him size her up and down. She was about five six if a centimeter, and a bit thick waisted. She figured she was an easy target. "I'd like to stay a few more minutes. Nothing will happen out here."

"Ma'am, you've picked the darkest part of this Grand Avenue Bridge to stand for your reminiscing. Anybody could sneak out of these shadows. Now, do you have a car?"

"Sure. It's a couple blocks down, by Millie's Drive-In."

"Millie's? Man oh man, don't you just love that place? Their tenderloins are the absolute best!"

She was amazed this kid could get so worked up over tenderloins. That's what he was right this moment, a big kid, instead of a man of the law. It made her smile.

"Those things, hmm!" Officer Iston shut his eyes. "Being on the force, and trying to stay in shape, I can't partake of them like I use to! Did you have one, ma'am? How bout those onion rings? That's some good Iowa cookin' there! Yea, buddy!"

She laughed at the young policeman. For these brief moments he forgot there was real crime about. And Millie's, when she was at Lutheran Hospital, her loving husband brought her some right before—

Officer Iston shook his head, which brought him back to the reality of the situation. His eyes were saucers. "Ok, look ma'am, this is what I'm going to do. I have about ten more minutes of my rounds here. I would prefer you walk with me, to the lit section of the bridge. After I complete my rounds I'll come back for you and walk you up to Millie's."

"All right, Officer Iston! I'll be waiting and thank you for your attention." She watched Officer Iston turn. He looked over six foot tall and husky. Grandmother indeed. She followed him to the center of the bridge.

"Now this should do it, ma'am. I'll be back before that big clock strikes twelve-fifteen." He gestured to the clock planted in the state capitol's golden dome.

"Yes, Officer, I will be here." She returned her eyes to the river. The air seemed crisper now. Perhaps more rain was on the way. Now where was she, before the good man in blue came upon her?

Being back was so strange. Everything looked the same, but time settled on it all. Her family was scattered. Her daughter was grown. Where had all the time gone?

Her daughter. She couldn't wait to see her! Would her baby recognize her? It had been so long since she left. But she would be face to face with her soon. How many times had they traveled the thirty or so miles to Des Moines to shop? How many times had they gone to her sister Mae's house so her baby could spend the weekend with her cousins?

She's always felt sorry that she and her baby's daddy couldn't give her a brother or sister. But the doctors said another pregnancy would be dangerous. When her angel was born, alive and healthy, she knew she was blessed by God.

The north wind pushed her back. It was getting colder, and flashes of lightening lit up the northern sky. It was almost time. It was almost time to see her baby.

"Hey, big momma! You want some lovin?" A voice sounded behind her. "C'mon momma, I'll take you all the way home!"

She turned and saw a bearded man leaning from the passenger side window. Whiskey dissected the air. She turned back towards the river.

"Ahh, look at that. Big momma's playin' hard to get. I'll show her what's hard. Ya like that, big momma? Ya want to have some big hard vanilla stick?"

Her eyes remained on the river and her lips shut.

"Hey, big momma, I'm talkin to ya! Maybe I need to get out and show big momma how to show some manners, eh boys?"

She heard the creek of the door open. Whiskey made its presence more known. Oh, how she hated the smell! It soured her stomach. A hand suddenly brushed against her elbow.

"Hey, big, black momma, look at me, I said. Ain't cha got no manners? I figured all you black girls knew how to treat a white man!"

Her gaze remained on the river. Lightening flashed closer.

"Ain't you gonna turn around?" The hand grabbed her arm. "I'm talking to ya girl!" The hand tried to turn her to face him. But failed, since the man that was attached to the hand, crumbled to the sidewalk.

"Get up you slime. Get your butt back in the car, or you and your buddy are going to jail." Officer Iston stood above him. "By the time I count to three, your butt better be in that car."

"You stupid pig! You nearly cracked my head open." Mr. Whiskey slurred as he rubbed the back of his head "I'm pressin' charges against you, pig!."

"Sure, ok, buddy. And I'll get you for attempted sexual assault, and oh, we'll throw attempting kidnapping onto it too, and that's on top of public intoxication. Let Perry Mason get you out of that. Now get in the car, pal."

She watched the man stumble into the car, and slam the door. The car's tires soon squealed down Grand Avenue.

"Now, ma'am, will you listen to me? I think it's time you let me walk you to your car. It's just not safe here. Come on, please, the weather seems to be changing again. You said your car was by Millie's, so let's get going." Officer Iston urged.

Even though she hated to admit it, the young officer was right. It had been dangerous, no matter who looked over her. "I was lucky you showed up. And you're right, it is about time to head back. So, Mr. Officer of the Law, let's go."

"I'm glad you listened to reason. Just not safe for anyone late at night, especially on a Friday, with the bars winding down."

Officer Iston stood on her left, protecting her from the street, as they began their walk to Millie's Drive-In. She bet Mrs. Iston was proud of the man her son became. She took one last look at the Des Moines River. The wind was much more brisk now, the roses' sweetness was abound. Clouds had covered the full moon. Yes, it was time.

'Ma'am, I've been calling you that for the last bit now. You know my name is Iston. Dion Iston. What's yours? I'd like to tell my mom I met another East High grad."

She chuckled softly. They'd stopped for the red light at Grand and Second Avenue. *"Officer, I mean, Dion, I doubt if she ever heard of me."*

"Oh come on, just tell me your name. She just might get a kick out of it anyhow. Me meeting another East High grad!"

As the light changed from red to green, she said, *"My name is Burscot. Frances Burscot. But, my maiden name was Wallace."*

Officer Iston, instinctively looked to his right and then to his left, before crossing. *"Wallace, eh? Hmmm. I'll tell mom that—hey? What's going on here? Ma'am?"*

When Officer Iston turned back to his right, to look at the woman he'd been walking and conversing with, there was no one beside him.

•✦•

Tonight was the eve of her wedding! Yes, tomorrow night, when the bell tolled seven, she, Lydia AnMarie Burscot, would do the unthinkable! Yes, she, Lydia AnMarie Burscot, on the cusp of the big four—oh, was tying the proverbial knot! Her dream of an October wedding was, at long last, a reality!

October, a flicker in time when leaves evolve from a gorgeous green to a ravishing red, mixed with the glimmer of gold! The air bestowed a wisp of crispness on an unsuspecting population. Everything changed *period* in October, so why shouldn't she?

Yes, she, Lydia AnMarie Burscot, planned to say her almighty 'I do's' with a fellow, who possessed her entire heart and soul. Coincidentally, he even possessed those same two things, when they both were just twelve years old. This very same fellow she hesitantly asked her mother about so many years ago. Maybe good things do come to those that wait, she thought.

After a particular Spring seventh grade day, Lydia raced home. She had to ask Mama a question. This was so very important! Tilda told Lydia not to be afraid to ask her Mama anything! Because Mrs. Burscot, knew everything—unlike Tilda's mom.

Tilda reminded her how cool Lydia's mom was! After all, didn't Lydia know all about her period before anybody else did? That alone, made Lydia the Queen of Know All Tell All, 'cause she told her friends, first hand, what it was like to wear those yucky, thick kotex. Yea, Lydia's mom was way cool, Tilda reassured.

Lydia's heart skipped a beat as she tried to stroll through the backdoor. She wanted to be as cool as possible, in front of Mama. Lydia leaned against the kitchen counter, just to the right of Mama. Lydia rested her chin on her right fist. She licked her lips. It was now or never.

"Mama—"

"So, Thomasina, how was school today?" Mama's fingers massaged floured noodles as her eyes sparkled at Lydia.

Lydia loved it when Mama called her Thomasina. It was from one of Lydia's favorite Disney movies about a cat with that name. Since Lydia loved cats, Mama always called her Thomasina, while the rest of Daddy's family christened her, Tom Cat.

"Well, it was ok, I guess. In English, Miss Marken wants us to write somethin' about some kinda adventure. I was thinkin' 'bout a lion gettin' away from a circus! Then they hafta shoot it with somethin' to get it back to the circus!"

"Sounds interesting, baby."

"But Mama, I wanna ask you somethin'—"

"There is a 'g' at the end of that word, girl!"

Mama had made noodles from scratch and now separated them with her now floured hands. Lydia wished her hands were as beautiful. Mama's hands were perfect! Mama put glossy frosty kind of nail polish on them. Mama always got mad at her because she picked at her nails. Lydia figured hers would never be as pretty, so why bother?

Nerves made goose bumps pop up on Lydia's arm. She shivered as noodles lie silently on wax paper. Lydia had to muster up guts to get her question out! She just had to! Lydia's devout attention now centered on Mama washing flour off her perfectly, frosty, polished hands.

"Thomasina, baby, what is it? Everything ok?" Mama's eyes became slits. That concerned line, between her eyebrows, appeared.

"Well, Mama, yea, I wanna ask a question. Hmm—" Lydia sputtered. She took a deep breath. Just spit out the rest, she commanded herself. "Mama, is it ok for me to like a white boy? I mean, would you and Daddy get real mad if I did?"

Mama was quiet for the longest, Lydia thought. It was an eternity! Had she gone too far? Was Mama gonna blow up at her? Sweat glued Lydia's fingers together. Lydia watched Mama tap the kitchen table with a perfectly, frosty polished nail. Was this the signal for Lydia to bolt or smile?

When Lydia felt no more breath could come inside her, Mama finally spoke. "Why, baby, yes, of course, you can like a white boy. Why do you ask? Why don't we sit on down at the table?"

Lydia wanted to pretend she didn't hear Mama's concern. For some reason, Holly Kevins appeared in Lydia's mind. Holly Kevins was the other black girl in Brenner Community Junior High. It was just the two of them in their class. Wonder if Holly Kevins was asking her parents the same exact question at the same exact time? A wave of panic washed over her.

Oh, who cares? Holly Kevins' mother was no where as cool as my Mama! Lydia thought. She was positive of that! If Holly

Kevins asked her mama such a question, she would certainly be sent to bed, after being ordered to eat a plate of nasty ol' asparagus! Holly Kevins' mama would hate to hear anything about a white boy or any boy for that matter!

Lydia pulled a chair from the kitchen table. "Well, I didn't want to make you and Daddy mad at me or anything!" Her voice shook. She twirled tips of her hair between her thumb and index finger. Lydia bit her bottom lip and silently prayed that Mama wasn't too mad at her, because she hated asparagus.

"We've got a few minutes before I go get Daddy. So let's talk about this."

Daddy would be tired from killing pigs all day at the pork plant. Half the town worked out there. The other half, like Tilda's dad, worked on the railroad. Wonder if he was so really, really tired and got mad at her? She couldn't stand Daddy being mad at her for anything!

Why doesn't Mama hurry up? wondered Lydia. She intently watched her mother wipe her hands on her apron, then sit on the chair beside her. Lydia was already positioned, sitting on her knees.

Lydia loved Seth, and had to know if it was ok. She sat, determined, not to miss a word Mama said! Every part of her tingled at the mere thought of him! His cute face. His cute smile. His cute everything! No offense to Mama, but Lydia wished she'd hurry up! Lydia bounced on her knees—time was wasting!

"Now, baby, I have to ask you—has a boy ever tried to touch you? On your private parts? Be honest with me." Mama's eyes pierced through her.

"Mommy, NO! Why would they want to? I see some look at my legs. Tilda says it's 'cause I wear such short dresses! But you told me to tell you if anything like that happened." Lydia nervously rocked her weight from knee to knee.

"If one ever does, I still want you to tell me right away! You're growing into a young lady. Your body is developing. Boys are looking you up and down now. They like the looks of your legs and breasts. The looking is fine—just as long as they aren't *mean and nasty about it, understand? Definitely no touching, ok?"*

Lydia nodded quickly.

"Good. You are becoming a young lady! You deserve treatment as such! Remember that!"

Lydia wondered where this part of the talk came from. All she wanted was to know if loving Seth was ok. Nonetheless, she knew she better listen. Mama knew everything.

"Boys are going to want to talk to you. And because they're white, that doesn't matter. And just because Tate Justin and his brother, Handly, are black, doesn't mean you have to like just them. Anybody can be friends with anybody. Don't you dare think otherwise, ya hear me? Don't you let anybody tell you otherwise either. Always use that gray matter that God gave you, remember that!" Mama's cinnamon scented words stung Lydia's face. "Daddy and I will not get mad at you liking a white boy, black boy, red boy, whatever—period! Just remember you are a young lady. You act as such. Understand?"

Lydia was breathless. Had Mama just given permission? Wow! Holly Kevins' mama would never be this cool! Lydia smiled. "So, it's—it's ok? You're not mad or anything, Mama?" Lydia's heart raced! This was turning into the best day of her life!

"Hmm—well, it will be ok, if you tell me the young man's name." Mama's tone softened. "This boy better be something special for you to be smiling like that, girl!"

Lydia's cheeks always flushed when Mama teased her. "Yes, oh yea, Mama, he's really, really cool!"

"Then don't keep me in suspense! What is this young man's name?"

The chance finally arrived for Lydia to say his beautiful name out loud. The whole world waited! Flowers of true love bloomed in her tummy. "Oh, Mama, his name is Seth Jacob Delaney!"

"Girl, you know the boy's whole name? Now how is that?"

"We went around the room one day in Miss Marken's, you know, she's my English teacher, and we had to say our whole complete name. And that was his! Isn't it cool? His birthday is January 18, too!"

"Oh no, Lydia, his birthday, too?" Now Mama laughed. *It was hearty and full of fun. Lydia loved the sound. "Ok, I guess it must be love! What else can you tell me about Seth Jacob Delaney?"*

"Well, he is so cute! He's got blond hair! An' wears these black glasses, an' plays Little League! An' he's on the same team as Richard Alan. They play for the Elk's Club." Her words ran, but she didn't care! She was not going to be denied. *"An' Tilda really likes Richard and I like Seth, an' they play tonight, down at Davis Park!"*

"The game starts at six, an' me an' Tilda wanna ride our bikes there. We'd still be home before dark. Can I? Can I? Tilda's gonna ask her mom, too! She's gonna call me. Can I? Can I?" Lydia found herself exhausted. How could she be tired? Mama just told her it was okay to like Seth.

Just then the phone rang. Daddy was ready to come home. As her mother picked up her car keys, she turned and looked at Lydia, *"Look, let me talk to Daddy about it. If we decide to let you go, it would be a better idea if I drove you and Tilda to the park. Daddy may want to fish after supper, so it could work out ok. Get the table set, and see you in a bit, baby."*

Lydia stood up as Mama walked toward the back door. When the door closed, Lydia spun around, filled to the brim with love. Lydia usually hated setting the table, but on this day, she danced as she put the silverware down by the plates. It made one less obstacle standing in the way of her casting her eyes on Seth Jacob Delaney.

She was going to see him play baseball tonight! Sure, she knew nothing about baseball, who cared? Seth was going to be there! Of course, he didn't yet know she existed and she would make sure that changed! She swore to that!

And there it began—her love affair with Seth. Unbeknownst to Seth, till twenty some years later!

Lydia eased from the car and scanned the darkness. Streaks of lightning broke up the far northern sky. A soft roar of thunder reached her ears. And where was she, Lydia AnMarie Burscot, on this night of nights? A night, her skin prickled from currents of frazzled nerves? A night where Mr. Sandman might be hesitant in his arrival?

Well, she stood on a patch of land in central Iowa, which ironically was smack dab in the center of Samm county. She was in the town of Brenner, population seven thousand, give or take, approximately thirty-five miles northwest of Iowa's capital city, Des Moines. More precisely, Lydia stood on the blessed grounds of Brenner's only cemetery, Violet Hill.

Lydia checked her watch and Ms. Timex informed her it was nearly eight. The wind, picking up speed and a chill, triumphantly whipped through her. She pulled her jacket's collar more securely around her neck. She glanced down at Jangles, her parents' gray schnauzer, sitting at her feet.

"Well, Jangles, rain is headed this way. Better not stay too long." Jangles responded with a short bark. "Come on, around the front."

She tugged his leash and he trotted beside her. He was a silly, spoiled little dog and she adored him! Her father, Dee, and step-mother, Jewel, spoiled him more than they spoiled her, but she didn't care! She had them both to celebrate her day of days with her.

Lydia's fingers ran through her black hair, attempting to undo the wind's damage. Another gust of wind informed her it was a lost cause. Lydia smiled, for nobody had to tell her how blessed she was! Lydia had Jewel to thank for handling most of the hometown plans, including reserving the Reverend Terry! And now Daddy was finally able to give her away. This *was* a dream come true.

Lightning separated the night sky again, as Lydia stood upon her destination. Raindrops dotted both her and Jangles, who immediately shook his furry body. Lydia's ever dampening right hand gripped Jangles' leash, while her left caressed the object of her destination.

Even with the rain, the marble headstone was rough to the touch. Lydia knelt beside it. The street's lamppost helped Lydia trace the carved letters on the stone's front:

FRANCES MARIE BURSCOT
July 9, 1928-Sept. 27, 1971
Here, rested Lydia's most wanted piece for her wedding day puzzle. *Mama.*

• ◆ •

On September 27, 1971, at five in the morning, thirteen year old Lydia was roused from her restless sleep by Daddy. His face bent close to hers, and by his expression—Lydia knew.
Baby, we don't have a mommy anymore.
Daddy's head fell to her chest. Lydia knew their lives would never be the same again. Tears had their way with her. She wanted to hang onto Daddy and believe this was a horrible nightmare. Daddy eased from her grip and Lydia saw his eyes were dry.
As the longest day of Lydia's short existence stretched on, tears were her constant companion. She seemed to cry at every turn. When the flowers arrived from her schoolmates, tears flowed so hard, she thought her eyes would fall out too.
Total strangers brought food that filled every nook and cranny of their kitchen. Who were these people? Where had they come from? Why were they in her house? Why was this happening to her? What had she done to God to deserve this? Pick at her fingernails too much? Not clean her room enough? Just what was it?
Daddy stood near. His big, strong arms made her feel safer. But Lydia knew she could never feel as safe as she had. Even as she did, a week ago. Mama was dead. Mama was in heaven. Daddy was her only foundation now.
Was it only yesterday that she was like any other regular thirteen year old? Hadn't she just gabbed, on her phone to Tilda? Then didn't they gallivant around town on their bikes? And play albums of their favorite group, the Osmond Brothers? Hadn't they both prayed for Seth and Richard Alan to glance their way in the hallways?

Now with the dawn of a new day, Mama's youngest sister, Rose, informed Lydia that yes, indeed, Lydia was now a woman. And why? Because Lydia knew where a box of Saltines lay hidden. There was more to being a woman, than knowing where crackers were. Mama taught her that.

Those first few days lasted longer than the scripted twenty-four hours each. Whenever possible, Lydia went into her parents' room and lie on Mama's side of the bed. Only a few days ago, she had been there. Alive.

Lydia replayed their final moments together, over and over. When Mama was still alive. When Lydia still had both parents telling her they loved her.

• ➤ •

It was September 24, a Friday. Lydia looked forward to telling Mama, about the absolute thrill of finally being part of the eighth grade. Which automatically made her part of the loudest grade at their first football pep rally of the season! Instead, on this day, Lydia watched paramedics prepare to take Mama from their home, strapped to a cot.

Lydia struggled to hold on to a more struggling Siamese cat, Minglee. Lydia searched Mama's eyes for some sign of hope. She was coming back, wasn't she? Mama attempted to pet Minglee—one last time. The cat howled because he sensed it too.

This couldn't be all there was ever going to be! Mama was coming home! Just like she did when the kidney stones were taken out. Mama had to come home! She just had to! Mama would have to be there to get on her about her fingernails. And the make-up, so she didn't over do it on the blue eye shadow and look like a blue jay again. Or tease her about Seth. Mama just had to come home!

Tears fought their way to freedom. Lydia held them at bay. There was no way, Mama was going to see her cry. No way! Mama taught her to be strong. Even when Mama said the words she dreaded to hear:

When I am not here, you're the woman of the house. Mama love.

Lydia knew there was no turning back. Not back to June, when she should have told Mama not to have the surgery. Mama taught her to never fight those feelings. Intuition, Mama called it. All women had it, Mama said. That was the one day Lydia didn't follow it, and now Mama was never coming home.

While Daddy and Mama rode the ambulance to Des Moines, Lydia sat in a bathtub of cold water and long dead bubbles. Aunt Grace waited for her in the living room. Lydia had protested she was too old for a baby-sitter. But this night, the fight was lost. With silent screams, prayers, and tears, Lydia demanded God, to spare Mama and take her instead. Why wasn't He listening?

Days became weeks, then months, and finally years. Lydia often dreamt of life if Mama had lived. How many times had she cursed God? Hoping to just wake up and be twelve years old again, dreaming of only Seth, and her next strawberry sundae from the Tasty Treat? Why her mother? What had Mama done to deserve this?

At times, the calendar in Lydia's mind said all this happened yesterday, instead of over twenty-five years ago. The ache softened, yet never went away.

•◆•

Jangles' barks snapped Lydia to the present. She wiped her damp cheeks. Were they damp due to tears, the rain or both? "What is it, boy? Smell something out here?"

Jangles stood directly across from her, on the other side of Mama's grave. In the dim light she saw his stub tail wag. This crazy dog made her smile. "We won't be out here too long, promise! Now what was that?"

Lydia turned her head over her left shoulder. She had heard a rustling sound hadn't she? Well, maybe not. Probably just wind running through remaining leaves on the trees. Lydia returned her attention to the headstone. She glanced at Jangles, who still stood on all fours, with tail still wagging. He barked twice, which made her laugh. "There's nothing out here, but you and me, you nut!"

At the same instant, both the rain and wind picked up their pace. Lydia realized she had to get whatever was on her chest off her chest. Fast. She pushed hair out of her face, and turned to the headstone. "Mama, I came out here earlier today. I just— Jangles! What are you doing?"

Jangles' barks turned into whines. Lydia watched the schnauzer rub his face twice against the headstone. Then he trotted the length of Mama's grave and back—twice. After his second trip, Jangles scratched the ground around the headstone.

"Stop that, Jangles! What do you think you're doing? You better not lift your leg on that!" Lydia snapped and yanked on his leash.

Jangles resisted and dug faster. As quickly as he began scratching, Jangles stopped and retraced his path, to the bottom of the grave. Lydia heard him whimper. What was all this? She called his name, yet he ignored her. His interest was only on the grave.

"Jangles! Come on! Stop! I'm the one that's here for business, not you! Not to watch you act all goofy!" Lydia settled herself, again, on her knees. She looked at Jangles, who gazed back at her. He stood at the bottom of the grave.

The wind gusted, while lightning signaled it was closing in. Time was slipping away and Lydia knew she must hurry. Jangles sounded threw three short yelps.

"Jangles, come here," she demanded. Lydia tugged gently on his leash. A surge of heat suddenly engulfed her spine. Was a fever coming on? Nope—not for her wedding! The surge subsided within seconds. Lydia tugged the leash again and this time Jangles didn't fight. He walked to the headstone, plopped on his belly, and shut his eyes.

"Jangles, I just don't get you!" Lydia sighed and cleared her throat. "Mama, I know I was here earlier today, but I had to come back. I had to. I'm getting married tomorrow! By this time tomorrow, I will have done the do! Can you believe it? I know you, Mary, Grace, and Hip will be front and center! But it just won't be the same. I know it hurts Daddy that his sisters and brother, and especially you, aren't here to share his joy." Lydia ushered tears aside. "I bet you guys knew before I did that I was going to marry Seth, huh? And Mama, he's the same little leaguer I asked you about those many years ago! I know I was a sight that day! You handled it beautifully. Just like you always did, when I posed those life type questions to you! For that, I'm very grateful!" Lydia heaved a sigh into the night air. "I know I'm a grown woman, yet at times, especially at night, I feel like a little girl waiting for you to tuck me in. Those are the times, I swear I feel you, Mama. Watching over me, watching me sleep. Also, when I was little, I remember you walking past my room, saying 'Mama love.' God, how I miss that! I was definitely safe from harm then! Mama, what kind of friends would we have become? Heaven knows, our shopping expeditions would have been front page material! Merle Hey Mall would never be the same!"

Lydia repeatedly ran her hand over her mother's name. The lump in her throat grew large. "My God, I'm getting married tomorrow! And you're not here! None of you! Dammit! Where were our talks of love and men? The laughter? Even the mistakes made along the way? Why did all of you have to go? Grace should be calming my nerves by hashing over our daytime stories. Mary ought to be mixing up a batch of her infamous biscuits while I still sit on that wooden stool alongside the counter. And Hip, oh Hippy, should be forever clamoring for his money on lost New Year's football games. And then lying about his fishing exploits. He said we had to fish at night, because fish supposedly bit better! I know he missed you most then! Being the fisherwoman you were." Lydia lowered her head. She covered her mouth with a trembling fist and choked on her tears.

Where's all the fish at, Uncle?" Lydia asked Hip.

They sat beside each other on the riverbank, at their favorite fishing hole in Adel. Daddy, always the solitary fisherman, sat a few feet away. The ever present King Edward cigar dangled from his mouth.

"Well, Tom Cat, I dunno. They all must be home, watching Johnny Carson!"

With that declaration, Lydia tossed her head back and cackled. Once Lydia regained her composure, the slow rush of the river was the only sound heard. "Hey, whatsa matter, Daddy? Hippy?"

"Ya know what, Dee?" Hip asked. "The way Tom Cat laughed, I woulda sworn Frances was sittin' on this riverbank!"

•◆•

Lydia let the headstone balance her as she sat on the ground. Her head rested against the stone, while raindrops trickled down her face. The rain, splashing on the headstone, sounded like a gentle heartbeat.

"Thirteen years was not enough time for anything. Ok, sure, maybe I'm being selfish. The only child thing in me. I just want everything my way and everybody I want around me on this day of days! But it's all I had. What is done is done. God had his plan, I realize that and I can't fight it. My love is always there for you, no matter what! Believe that!" Lydia stood up and brushed damp grass from her sweats and sighed. "The next time I'm out here, Mama, I shall be a married woman! And with a hyphenated name no less!" She tugged on Jangles' leash. "Ya ready to go sweety? Come on, little dog."

Jangles sprang to his feet and wagged his tail, yet resisted.

"Jangles, what is it? Jangles, come on!" She tugged again and he planted his four paws in the ground. Again. She was losing patience, with the hound, in a major big time way. "Jangles, rain is falling harder, come on! Jangles—Huh? What *are* you doing?"

Lydia watched as Jangles rubbed his head twice against the headstone, as he did before, but this time he balanced on his hind legs. Then he strolled across the grave, past Lydia, and stopped at the passenger door.

"Dog, I don't get you. I have to tell Daddy and Jewel about this. Come on, get in the car!" As Jangles hopped in the opened door, Another heat surge rushed her spine. At that precise moment, the night blew its cool breath, as if to bring down the temperature. The wave subsided as Lydia eased into her car.

As Lydia steered the car forward, rain pelted the windshield. "We got out of there in time, didn't we Jangles?" Jangles nudged her right arm with his nose. "You are more spoiled than me, if that's possible. I'm glad we live just a few blocks from here!"

A flash of lightning engulfed the car, blinding her. Claps of thunder shook the earth. Lydia instinctively eased her foot from the gas pedal. "Oh, my God, that was something! That even scared me! I couldn't see anything! But we're ok, huh, Jangles?" Lydia reached over and petted the gray schnauzer. He responded by licking her hand.

As Lydia exited Violet Hill's gate, she thought, out of the corner of her eye, she saw two shadows standing by some head-stones. Probably just the branches, hanging down, she thought.

• ◆ •

On a particular eighth grade afternoon, a month after Mama left, Lydia and Tilda skipped their way home, from Brenner Junior High. Rain suddenly started falling. They laughed and splashed. Lydia always felt better when she and Tilda were together.

Lydia knew she had Daddy and his side of the family, but hated to admit that she still got lonely sometimes. Mama's side of the family didn't come around much at all.

It didn't help that her twin cousins, Starr and Wallace, had moved to Arizona with their mother Mae, who was Mama's oldest sister. They had packed up and headed West only a month before Mama left. Mama planned to ride an airplane, for the first time, so she could visit them in Arizona. She never made it.

Lydia missed going to Des Moines and spending weekends with Starr. She was the big sister Lydia never had. They played

Barbies, talked boys, and contemplated whether or not they really could get drunk off the Champagne Ice at Baskin-Robbins. Now Starr was a galaxy away and a big hole remained.

The rain freed Lydia. It made time stand still. As if nothing had ever happened. As if Mama never left.

The two best friends frolicked in the rain, until its magic unceremoniously vanished. Lydia let the rain cleanse her, until Tilda's mom drove up and ordered them into the car.

Lydia's blue sweater, totally drenched, bled into the white turtleneck underneath it. If Mama were still here, Lydia knew her butt would be beet red. To have Mama back, she would take the spanking.

Lydia opened the house's front door and the first notes, of the *Bonanza* theme, greeted her. Understanding Daddy and Jewel's love for westerns was beyond her, and she loved teasing them about it.

Instead of trotting to her parents' room, when he was unleashed, Jangles dashed up the attic steps. The same attic where her wedding gown hung, protected in plastic.

"You better not do anything to that dress, you mutt!" Lydia was confident Jangles had no access excess to it.

"Lyd? Is that you?" Jewel asked from their bedroom. "Did you and Jangles get very wet?"

"Naw, just a little. Rain's coming down pretty good now." Lydia hung up her jacket and headed to the kitchen. Being back in Brenner, she needed her almost daily fix of Tasty Treat ice cream. The Tasty Treat ice cream ranked up there with the ritual of Cheeseburger Hamburger Helper.

In the beginning, right after Mama left, she and Daddy devoured so much of the macaroni, cheesy hamburger stuff, they should have owned stock! Even to this day, whenever Lydia visited, Daddy whipped up a batch. It was their ritual, and this wedding trip made it no different.

Suddenly, two loud barks sounded.

"Whatsa matter with the devil dog?" Dee asked.

"Hmm. I don't know. He shot up the steps to look at my dress. Which I'm going to do shortly!" Lydia entered their bedroom, spooning her mouth with vanilla ice cream.

Jewel was in bed, propped against pillows, while Daddy reclined in his favorite blue chair. Both had been glued to the adventures of the Cartwright family. Lydia rolled her eyes and then centered them on her father.

Daddy was now in his early seventies. Age slowed him down in some ways, yet in others, Lydia saw the same man who taught her the path to Webster Elementary School. There he would fill her mind with adventures destined for her, in kindergarten. They peeked into the school's window where, Lydia had never seen such long tables before! Daddy told her how much fun he had in kindergarten, a long, long time ago, and she would have the same. Lydia was sure Daddy told her the truth. He always told the truth! So if school was going to be a lot of fun, it would be!

The last leg of their walk was always Lydia's favorite! They would walk past the line of apple trees on Seventh Street. Since Lydia was small, Daddy hoisted her up so she could pick them a couple. By that time, Mama worked during some afternoons. To make sure Mama wouldn't feel left out, Lydia made sure she picked an extra special apple for her.

Lydia smiled because earlier in the day, she and Jangles journeyed down that very same street and past those same apple trees. Age had taken a toll on them too, just like Daddy. Next Spring, Lydia reminded herself, she must check if they still bore fruit. If they did, and since she was tall enough now, she would pick a couple for Daddy and her.

"Girl, what you doin' with that ice cream? You gonna fit in that dress tomorrow? I hope your butt ain't too big!" Daddy teased, as he took his cigar out of his mouth.

Lydia groaned. "Has anything been said about the rain stopping?'

"Anyway, the weatherman said should clear out by daybreak. Just be cold as hell and give me a taste of that there ice cream."

Lydia handed him a spoonful.

"Dee! You know what the doctor said!" Jewel always got after him, since his diabetes, caused amputation of his left foot two years ago.

"Woman, it's only a spoonful! And you know my damn blood is good!" Dee gruffed back.

Jewel permitted him to be monarch occasionally and this was one of those times. Lydia laughed at their exchange. Jewel sighed, shook her head, and turned her attention to Lydia. "So TZ gave you ice cream, huh? What has he had to say about you getting married, baby?"

Lydia knew what Jewel was getting at and immediately shoveled more ice cream into her mouth. Once upon a time, specifically during her late teen years, TZ was the love of her life. Heck, she'd picked out names for their kids! After all, TZ was the first guy who said he loved her, and she believed him.

Just a few years ago, TZ admitted they should have married. When asked why it never came to pass, TZ claimed he couldn't provide the life she deserved. Financially wasn't the problem, emotionally was. Lydia knew he was right, for personal demons held him captive.

Eventually, and with much difficulty, Lydia found the power to move on. The love affair may have ended, but the fact he ran his family's Tasty Treat business, always made her come back.

"Well—" Lydia's voice drifted. Jewel's charcoal eyes zeroed in on her. "He says he wants me to be happy. And of course, we'll always be friends." A spoonful of vanilla ice cream made its way into her mouth. Much easier not to talk that way!

"Baby, you were so crazy about him!" Suddenly Jewel laughed loudly. "Remember that Christmas, he pulled his truck up in the yard, and gave your dad a shot of that—what was that, he gave you Dee?"

"A shot of piss. Hundred proof piss!"

"Dad! Dee!" Laughter poured into the room.

"Well, I gotta admit, it did burn a hole in my stomach!" Lydia announced.

"See, what did I tell you? A royal, hundred proof piss!"

"Donald! Please!" Jewel demanded. "You don't have to be so loud about it! But the look in your eyes when you tasted it-" Jewel laughed again.

That, indeed, had been a festive night! After all this time, Lydia still held onto that Christmas card TZ gave her. A guilty pleasure filled her whenever she pulled it from its secure hiding place. Though time passed, the memory still made her smile. "Since I'm going to be a married woman, TZ said I need to get use to paying for everything!"

"And you know he's talking out his head! We'll still get our strawberry sundaes. That is what we get, isn't it, baby?"

Lydia nodded.

"Hey, you better watch your ass, Jewel, or it's gonna break the bed. Eatin' all that ice cream and junk!" Those words had been enough ammunition for Dee.

"Donald, I think you better keep your mouth shut!"

Dee and Lydia both giggled. Jewel was grand at setting herself up.

As Lydia savored the dollops of ice cream, *Bonanza* was riding off into the sunset and snores escaped from Jewel's mouth. Lydia stole a glance at Dee, who was wide awake, with the King Edward situated between his lips.

Daddy and Jewel had been together more than twenty years. Didn't seem possible, he could have been with anyone else, but he had.

"Ya ready for tomorrow baby?" Dee asked in a soft voice.

"Yea, I guess so. I'm a little scared." Lydia paused and inspected her empty dish. She then looked and met her father's eyes. "Did you feel this way when you married Mama? Scared, I mean?" Lydia bit her bottom lip.

She watched her father lean back in his chair and the King Edward switched to the other side of his mouth. When conversations centered on Mama, black clouds rose above them. The passing years had only reduced their size.

"Yes, I was. But I knew it was the right thing to do. I was ready to get married. Is that how you feel? About Dumbo?"

Always the jokester, this Donald Edward Burscsot! Lydia was sure Daddy liked Seth, at least she hoped he did! In person, Daddy addressed Seth by his first name. But in private, he called Seth whatever his fancy fancied. Seth admitted her father intimidated him—just a little. Lydia figured it was probably Daddy's goal anyway.

"Yes, I do love him. I adore him! He's so good to me. Honestly, though, Daddy, does it bother you that Seth is white? I asked that same question to mom a long time ago."

"Baby, I've just wanted you to be happy. That's all. I've always told you that." His voice remained light.

Lydia relished these times. Just the two of them together. They'd been through a lot. Not always good, yet they survived. Cheeseburger Hamburger Helper and all.

"So if you still wanna marry Dumbo, I can't stop you!" Dee grinned.

"Of, *Father*, really!" She could tell Daddy wanted to lighten the mood.

"Hey, where did you and the dog go anyway?"

"Oh, Jangles and I took to the cemetery. I wanted to say good night to everybody and make sure they'd be at the wedding.

Jewel's snores stopped as *Wagon Train* galloped onto the screen. "What'd they say? Are they gonna make it?"

"Yea, they said they would try." Lydia began. "Hip's glad it's late in the evening so he won't miss the Iowa game!"

All three laughed. Hip was a bear, a gentle one, though, when it came to his sports.

"Well, I'm off to phone my soon to be husband. I need to make sure he's all set for tomorrow! Then I'm hittin' the trail to bed. See you guys in the morning!"

"Night, night baby. See you in the morning." Dee said as Lydia bent down to kiss him goodnight.

Lydia placed her empty dish in the sink, and sauntered toward the attic's steps. She planned to torture Seth about her gown. This gown, ivory and delicate lace, with sequins and jeweled stones, was exquisite!

In actuality, the gown's cost was more than they budgeted. Yet, from the moment Lydia spotted it, she knew she had to somehow have it! Because she was so heartsick, Seth, a man who counted pennies on any ninety-nine cent menu at any fast food joint, bought it for her, sight unseen.

Lydia knew she had herself one special man! She pictured the moment, Seth would first lay eyes on her, wearing it. She laughed as she pictured Seth's mouth crashing through the floor! If just the dress conjured such a reaction, what would the wedding night lingerie do? That thought made her flush. Almost like the rush of heat that doused her spine. *Almost.*

• ◆ •

Even through plastic, the gown shimmered. Moonlight waltzed with the sequins and stones perfectly. Lydia sat cross-legged on the floor and through the plastic, caressed the gown's hem. She smiled when she glanced at a snoozing Jangles, stretched out on the plastic's excess.

Lydia dialed the number, silently praying Seth would answer. His mother, wasn't clicking to the notion of Lydia being daughter-in-law material! Even if she were *white*, Lydia was sure that wouldn't even make a difference! Seth and she overcame quite a few obstacles, on their road to happiness. Perhaps in time, Mrs. Delaney would be another notch in their belt buckle.

Lydia heaved a sigh of relief when Seth's familiar voice came over the phone line. Her plan of attack was successful. Seth was such a good sport. Their conversation ended with giggles, coos, and whispers about their life together. After all this time, this guy still made her feel giddy.

When Lydia laid the phone down, heat seized her spine again. What was that? She wasn't feverish, so it just had to be nerves. Lydia looked at Jangles, who still snored away. He hadn't stirred an inch during her chat with Seth. So unlike the hound. His actions at the cemetery replayed in her mind. Surely, he wasn't sick. Hopefully, Jangles would be his ol' rambunctious self by morning.

Speaking of morning, Lydia glanced at her watch. This go-round, Ms. Timex showed her it was now a quarter to ten. Lydia inhaled deeply and shut her eyes. Her body started to relax. Tomorrow, no matter how glorious, destined to be a long day. Thank heaven, everything was scheduled to the letter, courtesy of Jewel.

The major event, outside of the actual wedding, was becoming Cinderella. That transformation would commence at two in the afternoon. Lacy, a friend since the fourth grade, when they got caught passing notes, and now owner of her own beauty shop, would wave the magic curling wand and spread the hair spray.

Lydia released a contented sigh. With knees drawn to her chest, she wrapped her arms around them. Lydia continued to inspect her gown. It radiated its own aura—so mesmerizing! Yes, tomorrow was going to be glorious indeed!

·◆·

Lydia stood up and shook sleep from her legs. She gently nudged Jangles. He lifted his head and looked at her. "Come on, boy we need to get ready for bed! Better let you out for a minute to do your business. The rain's stopped. Fresh air will do us both good!"

Without hesitation, Jangles ran down the steps and waited patiently by the front door. He seems ok now, Lydia thought.

Outside Lydia savored the night air. It smacked of an innocent clean. Anything disagreeable with the world, had been rinsed away. Everything was fresh and new again. Everything had changed again. Just the way Lydia relished.

Sleep would have no problem finding her now, she thought. A hand covered her yawning mouth. "C'mon Jangles, I'm ready to turn in." Lydia climbed into her favorite flannel nightshirt and began her nightly chore. First, out with the contacts, then washing off the make-up.

Once upon a time, during her high school years, no cosmetics made it to her eyes. No way at all! Even for her senior picture, Daddy nearly had to *pay* her to just dab on mascara. Then Tilda practically had to tie her down to do that! Just apparently some rebel with a cause, she laughed.

Jangles, guarding the bathroom door, perked his ear up when he heard Lydia laugh.

"Ya know, Jangles, I'm surprised there's anything left on my face. The way I balled out there, and with this rain."

Jangles responded by sneezing.

As Lydia smoothed moisturizer over her cleansed face and throat, she thought of her mother. Mama was great about using Noxema to cleanse her face. Oh, how she loved teasing Mama that the white sticky cream looked like shortening! And Mama just let her go on, until the day of reckoning.

That day showed up sometime during seventh grade. If Lydia wished to wear make-up, Mama announced, the ways of Noxema would have to be learned. Everyone was wearing *some* kind of makeup, and Lydia didn't want to be left out. So for the chance to wear robin egg blue eyeshadow, she and Mama became sisters in Noxema.

After things settled down from the wedding, Lydia promised herself, to check the shelves for Noxema. Just like the apple trees, if the thick cream was still around, she'd get a jar, just for old times sake!

Lydia wondered how different things would've been if Mama lived to ride buckshot during her wedding day? Disagreements would bounce from wall to wall, just like a basketball during the NCAA Tournament, but once the final buzzer buzzed, Lydia sensed everyone would be on the same winning team. That's the way it had been with Jewel.

She adored Jewel, no doubt there, yet vacancy, nonetheless, remained in her heart. Through the years, Jewel and she formed a strong bond, after some predictable, turbulent times. But a friendship, with Mama, her *real* Mama, how close would the two of them be? A question never to be answered, and that's sad, thought Lydia.

Lydia snuggled beneath the bedcovers after fluffing one of the two pillows. Jangles claimed his spot on the other. No bother to switch out the light. Daddy would do that eventually. Whenever home, Lydia drifted to sleep with the light on. Sometimes on purpose, sometimes not. In the mornings, Daddy informed her the time he shut the light off, how the ground shook because of her snoring, and how the neighbors complained. This was another delight of coming home—just like Tasty Treat ice cream and Cheeseburger Hamburger Helper. This was the good life.

•◆•

What was that? Was Jangles barking? Lydia sat up in bed and rubbed sleep from her eyes. The bedroom light was still on. Daddy hadn't made it in yet. Her nearsighted eyes attempted to focus on the digital clock. The red numbers, blurred as they were, looked like they said midnight. Why was this hound barking?

Strange, neither Daddy nor Jewel were yelling at him to stop. With glasses on, Lydia's cleared vision concurred with her blurred vision—it was midnight. Dumb dog. Why wasn't he asleep, like the rest of the animal kingdom?

Lydia tiptoed to peek on her parents. Light, from the TV, flickered about the room along with dialogue between Marshall Dillon and Miss Kitty. Snores rose from them both. They were totally oblivious to Jangles' barking.

Backing out of her parents' room, Lydia heard Jangles yelp twice. What was he doing upstairs? She'd just go get him, quiet him, then scurry back to her comfy bed. Fatigued filled her more than she realized. How dare this little gray mutt disturb her?

Lydia stood, with hands on her hips, at the bottom of the attic steps, "Jangles, what are you doing up there? Jangles?" Terror awakened her fully. What if Jangles got hold of her gown? "Jangles, if you've done anything to that dress, you are cat food! Do you hear me?"

The gown's condition took priority. Lydia stepped on the first step. Jangles, still unseen, barked louder and faster. Lydia noticed the attic's light was on. Strange. Hadn't she turned it off after talking to Seth? She was sure she had. But since light floated down the stairs, with her busted nerves, she evidently forgot.

"Jangles, come on down! I'm not playing!" For some reason, Lydia froze on the third step. What was the big deal? She'd been up these steps, zillions of times. Zillions. So why did her body stiffen and feet freeze to the carpet?

"You little mutt, where are you?" Her right foot, thawed, suddenly weighed a ton as she lifted it to the fourth step. Eight more steps beckoned her. Lydia felt dizzy and shut her eyes. She leaned against the wall for support and licked her now dry lips. She slowly opened her eyes and saw Jangles standing at the top of the stairs.

His stub of a tail wagged rapidly. The light appeared more brilliant. Where did Daddy buy these lightbulbs?

"Jangles, your stupid barking woke me up! Get down here!"

Jangles stretched and directed a yawn at her.

"Come on—NOW!"

Instead of giving into demand, Jangles concluded his stretch, turned, and sauntered from view.

Lydia heard him bark four times. "Jangles, stop that!" Any dizziness or whatever happened—passed. "Ok, Jangles, I'm coming to get you! That gown better be in one piece! If you whizzed on it, your new address is the pound!" Lydia found confidence to march up the remaining steps.

All she had to do was kill the dog, and flip off the light. Not a problem. Ready for step twelve, she heard Jangles whimper. "Jangles? Now what? You ok?" What was that? Heat ran up her spine again. Was she that nervous?

Lydia stepped onto the carpet. Her eyes widened, as she looked straight ahead, at the attic's light switch. It was in the 'off' position. How could that be since the room was completely illuminated?

What in the world was going on? Beads of sweat formed on her forehead. She grasped the railing for support. Her wedding dress hung in the corner behind her. Without turning, she knew the light's splendor came from that corner. Her feet froze again. Somehow she managed three steps, and passed Mama's oak desk. Stalled in slow motion, Lydia turned toward the corner. Numbness replaced the heat in her back.

Ten feet away, her gown hung, and Jangles sat beside it. His gaze was upward, not at Lydia's gown, but at the *person* touching her gown! The subject of Jangles' attention was the light's source.

Lydia massaged her temples, yet no relief came. She ran a set of fingers through her hair. Why wouldn't her head clear? Jangles' yelp made her jump. Her eyes wandered from his furry body to the person blocking her view. How and, more less, *who* could be possibly standing here? This person, draped in white, was outlined in gold. The features, told Lydia, this person, was female.

Lydia watched a creamy, caramel hand caress the gown's satin sleeve. Where had the plastic covering gone? The woman's fingers then inspected the lace and jeweled beads, on the neckline. All the while Jangles sat intently beside their visitor, and seemed to smile. His tail continued to wag.

The woman's hair, velvet black, dusted her shoulders. Her fingernails donned a frosted, gloss polish. So very familiar, Lydia thought. Almost, as if on cue, Lydia again felt heat rise in her back. Dizziness and nausea made their presence known. This was stuff of Stephen King novels, not real life. Not *her* life! No way!

Lydia wanted to speak—yet words stalled deep in her throat. She swallowed hard. Maybe that would help and why was she so cold? Where was that heat when she needed it?

"It's about time you got here. I figured this hound's barking would wake the entire neighborhood."

That voice. No. No. It couldn't be. Lydia stepped back, grabbing the edge of the desk Breath escaped her, and refused to return. Lydia threw her free hand over her heart and clenched.

• ◆ •

"This gown is exquisite! You will be magnificent! What does your daddy say? Be his prettiest girl? Yes, that you will definitely be."

The uninvited female visitor had yet to turn around. Lydia shivered as she watched the woman's hands caress the sides of her gown, then trace the waistband seam.

That voice. Sounded so familiar. Could it be? No, Lydia thought. It's been decades since that voice sang to her. Lydia regained enough consciousness to inhale again. She knew she had to find who this woman in white was.

Jangles diverted his eyes, toward Lydia, just for a moment, then his attention returned to their visitor. His stub of a tail never stopped wagging.

"Why didn't I just leave you alone? Why couldn't I be happy—to let you be you? Isn't that what Dee and I taught you? Yes, you were overweight, yet, for the most part, you seemed comfortable. And that's what really mattered. Being a quote un quote, average size was something I wanted for myself and tried to force on you—" the woman's voice trailed off and Lydia heard her sigh. "If I'd had a clear head, I wouldn't have served asparagus. I made you sit at the table till you nearly cried. And you know something? I hated asparagus just as much! I only did it because it seemed like the healthy thing to do. Ha! Needless to say, we never had it again. No matter what healthy sign of the times idea I had, you still wound up with the best set of legs! Oh, how you loved wearing those purple hotpants! You thought you were so grown and twelve years old yet!"

That laugh. No way in the world or *Heaven*, could this be! Could it? Lydia managed baby steps toward the woman and stood directly behind her.

Lydia guessed the woman was an inch or two taller. A hint of some long forgotten fragrance also drifted from her. It conjured up images from the first new days of Summer. What was its name? Unfortunately, the years had wiped her memory clean.

Lydia bit her lip, it was now or never. Her right hand trembled as she reached for the woman's shoulder. Lydia's eyes widened as the outline of gold grew brighter. Her shaking hand was now shaking on the woman's right shoulder.

•◆•

"M-Mama?" Lydia whispered. "Oh my God, is it really you?" With her hand, Lydia guided the woman to face her. The eyes, the smile, the scent. Lydia's entire body trembled. Tears dripped from her eyes. Both of her hands flung over her mouth.

"Yes, baby, it's me. I had to see you. My angel is getting married!"

This being, this woman, this *ghost* was her mother, Frances Marie Wallace Burscot. Mama. Death had snatched her away over twenty-five years ago. Yet, this woman, resembled her forty-three year old mother, exactly as Lydia remembered. The *same* Mama—she snapped photos of, under their own apple tree, with their kitty, Minglee. That woman was forty-three. Forty-three! Just three years more than Lydia.

Lydia's search for a voice came up hoarse. "How? H-how did you get here? I mean, you're dead!"

"Why yes, dear, I realize that!"

Now how much more dumb could I be? Mama certainly did not arrive on the last American Airlines flight tonight. She's been dead since 1971! If this was truly happening, only the Hand of God could do such a thing. Suddenly, Lydia remembered that her parents slept below. "They might hear us! Jangles was barking—"

"They're fine. We won't disturb them, I promise. You look shaky. Let's sit a minute."

Lydia felt a hand take hers and permitted herself to be led to one of the attic's beds. The touch was as warm as the sensations Lydia experienced in her back.

"Oh, and the heat in your back? Yes, those were courtesy of me. For awhile, it was the only way I could let you know I was near."

"What? The heat? I don't —"

"Baby, you're getting married in a few hours! That gown is wonderful! The color is marvelous for you! You will be truly spectacular! You were always destined to be a beautiful bride!"

Lydia sat in amazement as she witnessed something she hadn't seen in years, Mama's smile. She felt guilty for not remembering how bright that smile actually was. It was as wonderful as the light that engulfed her. Lydia waited anxiously for her mother to continue.

"Now, for the reason I'm here. We missed so many things, my dearest Thomasina."

"Thomasina? Oh my god! I haven't heard that since I was twelve years old! I'd forgotten how good that sounded! Mama—"

Fingers were pressed to Lydia's lips. "Baby, please let me tell you something."

Lydia closed her mouth. She always had to make sure she listened to Mama. Mama knew everything.

"All those times you came to Violet Hill to see us, *all* of us— I wanted to reach out and hold my baby. I loved those moments! Everyone enjoyed those moments, even those that frightened you when you were little!"

Lydia's hand was squeezed tighter. "What? Everyone? Huh? "Who do you mean?"

"Yes, your aunts, Grace and Mary, your uncle Hippy, even your dad's parents. And you didn't have the chance to ever know them. Then the man with the cows. Remember, how you hated walking past them, especially by yourself?"

"Old Morehouse Benston? Oh my goodness! That field, where he had his cows, now has the new elementary school on it!" Lydia was surprised her body relaxed. "And, oh my, one year during my Blue Bird candy sale, I opened a box of candy, ate a piece, put the lid back on it, and sold that box to him!"

Was Mama really laughing with her?

"I had to unwrap the plastic to just to open the candy. I hated him so much, so I thought—big deal! Hey, I still got my dollar! The next year, though, Ol' Morehouse wondered why there was plastic on the box he held in his hand and none on last year's box! I about peed my pants!"

"Lydia! We never taught you to use that word!"

Lydia hoped she heard pretend frustration in Mama's voice and searched for clues. There was a familiar, vibrant fire in these dark eyes. "I was sure he was going to tell on me!"

"He did."

"What? And you didn't say anything? What I did was just cause for one of your whippings!"

"Under normal circumstances, you're right!" Lydia watched a devilish grin cross her mother's face. "But *I* never liked ol' Morehouse either!"

The room filled with the women's laughter. Jangles, curled against Frances' feet, looked up and cocked his head. With a sneeze, his head returned to its former position, and he shut his eyes.

Frances quieted first and cupped Lydia's right cheek. The touch made Lydia smile. After all these many years, Mama was touching her! Just like she use to! Lydia clasped her mother's wrist. The forgotten scent floated from her wrist, into Lydia's soul. Mama's skin was just as lovely and smooth as she remembered.

When she was little, Lydia told everyone that Mama had orange skin. Even now, Lydia saw how she got that notion and smiled. This face, Mama's face, had not been touched by age nor death. How beautiful! Without hesitation, Lydia kissed her mother's cheek, then cradled her head in the nape of her neck. "Mama? I thought I would never say that again!"

"Well, I got news for you—I thought I would never *hear* it again!"

Lydia knew she was safe in these wrapped arms. The moistness of Mama's lips pressed against her forehead. "This is unbelievable! I could ask for no greater wedding gift. Or gift period!"

Her wish of waking up and being twelve years old again had come true. Lydia was again that seventh grader rushing home to ask Mama about Seth. Before everything changed. Before Mama left. Before she was forced to be an adult. Lydia huddled closer, for this moment could not be lost.

"Baby, at night, I've been near and you've felt my presence."

Lydia was confused and could muster no words.

"Think about it baby. Remember nights, when a cool breeze seemed to roll over you, and there was no open window in sight?

Lydia nodded, too afraid to speak.

"It was right before you drifted off. My hands helped you pull the covers over you. I had to make sure my baby was protected."

"I-I don't know. I always wanted to believe that you—"..

Frances squeezed Lydia's hands. "And tonight, at Violet Hill, words and thoughts brought me here. They've always brought me to you! God permitted this night, just the two of us."

"But, Mama, why now? Why after all these years?"

"Because," Frances smiled, "you're getting married! My angel is getting married! A mother must be there to share her daughter's extra special moments. And there are others, that also love you, who want to be a part of your special day."

Lydia sat straight and wiped away her tears. "W-who are you talking about?"

"Baby, I'm speaking of your aunts and uncle! When you watch your stories, Grace and Mary are both right there! And Hippy is with you through all four quarters of any football game."

"Oh, my goodness! That makes me feel so good. Sometimes I catch myself talking out loud during those soaps. I expect a response any second. Maybe I did feel something!" Lydia wiped her eyes again. "I'm speechless. I really don't know what to say, except, I'm afraid I'm going to wake up! I've prayed to see you. Talk with you. So many things." Lydia squeezed one of her mother's hands.

"And this little guy?" Frances scratched the top of Jangles' head. "I think he's part of a past pet. Maybe Minglee. Oh, how I adored that cat!"

Lydia watched her mother smile. Had it always been so bright? "Hmm, yes, I recall how much you loved that cat. I also recall how ticked I was because I wanted to name him Max and you said it wasn't Siamese enough! Geesh!" Lydia rolled her eyes.

Frances giggled. "Ah, yes I remember! He did look like a Minglee, and besides mother does know best, dear!"

"Well, Mama, I see sarcasm does run in the family!"

"Oh, like mother, like daughter, eh? Is that what you're saying, Thomasina?"

Lydia sighed and nodded. Unfortunately Mama hadn't lived long enough for Lydia to appreciate her tone.

"Enough on that. Let me say more about you being at Violet Hill tonight, I know Jangles frightened you with his grave dance. He felt my presence, while you could—"

"Only feel the heat up my back?" Lydia finished.

"Yes, baby. Now right this moment, for the first time in eternity, I can actually hold my one and only!" Frances lifted Lydia's chin with a finger. "We have so much to talk about. You have feelings, perhaps even anger, that have built up for so many years. I want to hear it all! But first, Lydia, let me reassure you. I always loved you. Always." Frances pinched Lydia's chin between her fingers.

"This can't be happening. I've wanted this for so long—"

"Baby, I hated leaving you. It was difficult for you and your dad. All those years—" Frances' voice and eyes both lowered.

Lydia's stomach twisted into knots. A war suddenly began to rage and overthrow her serenity. Lydia's body trembled and grew cold.

She now sat at Mama's side. A place she'd yearned and cried for, through so many nights. But, truthfully, back on that September morning in 1971, this same person—a person who said she loved her—had left her alone. Only to return, in flat photographs and blurred memories. Until now—

The ice of Lydia's body ignited red heat. Her pulse raced and the desire to scream was immense. Lydia swore she heard the pounding of her own heart. Would it burst? Her left hand flew over her mouth. Words, gargled in her throat, destined to be spewing lava. Their rage singed her throat.

How could she do this? Not to Mama! Not *now*! Lydia jerked to a standing position. Her feet became lead. Lydia shut her eyes and silently commanded her feet to move. She wrapped her arms around her and digested gallons of air.

Lydia made sure her back remained to her mother. Oh, how she wanted to calm down! To enjoy this moment. This *miracle*. Her body was a thermometer and the mercury raced to the burst the bulb.

Without hesitation, Lydia spun to be face to face with her mother. Lydia was shocked to see an index finger, *her index finger,* sit on her mother's nose. "Why did you go? Did you really have to die? We went through, hell, Daddy and I! How could you not know that? You knew that. *You knew that!* You left us! You left ME!"

Lydia thought her own eyes would fry in her skull. Oh, how she wanted to control herself, but the venom continued to surge. "I've always thought it was my fault you died! If I had told you not to have that damn surgery, you would be here, today, helping me plan my wedding. Oh but no, you went ahead with it! Over the years, Daddy told me you planned to go through with it, no matter what anybody said! Not until I was much older, did I finally believe him! Or I should say, I tried to believe him! Well, tell me something, *mother*, now, would me telling you my feelings, on the surgery, made any kind of difference? Would it? Would my feelings have been enough for you to not kill yourself?"

Lydia reached for air. Her head suddenly weighed a hundred pounds. As the room spun on its axis, focusing on anything was impossible. Just as quickly as the rage began, it subsided. Lydia had enough power to lower her head.

•◆•

Lydia heard the mattress creak. She knew Mama rose from the bed. That long forgotten scent made its way through her senses again. Lydia felt herself being pulled to her mother. Upon contact, tears spilled from Lydia's eyes and dampened her mother's celestial gown.

"Lydia, honey, there would have been no difference. None. I was determined—"

"I knew you would be gone by Christmas!" Lydia interrupted. "I knew it! That day we came out of the doctor's office—after your final check up. It was June, do you remember? Oh my god, you were so happy! So happy!"

Lydia pulled away from her mother's grasp and walked to the attic's open window. The autumn breeze dried her face. How in the world could this be happening? Lydia blinked, and cleared her vision. Perhaps, when she turned around, she would discover this was only a dream. There was no way Mama could be standing in the very same room with her. Absolutely none.

"Lydia? Lydia?"

This has got to be a dream! Please! I have to wake up. There was a hand on Lydia's right shoulder.

"Baby, please turn around. Look at me. Please"

Lydia shut her eyes. If this was a dream, the end was not near. Deep inside her soul, Lydia knew this to be true. The touch on her shoulder soothed her. Lydia, with arms crossed over her chest, opened her eyes and slowly turned toward the voice. Lydia wished not to look into her mother's eyes. Again she lowered her head.

"That day, coming from the doctor's office, Mama, you told me how skinny you were going to be! At that precise moment, I knew you were going to die. I thought I was going to puke. I knew you wouldn't be here for Christmas." Lydia rubbed her cheek with the back of her right hand. She made herself look into her mother's eyes. They looked sad. "Kinda funny, huh? Every kid usually can't wait for Christmas. And there I was, in the month of June yet, praying for that day to never arrive. I knew and I didn't stop you!" Lydia covered her face.

"Lydia, look at me! Look at me!" Lydia's hands were gently pried from her face, they were held tightly.

Their eyes met. *Am I the little girl she left behind? Or am I the grown woman she dreamt me to be?*

"Lydia, you couldn't have stopped me. I was determined. The surgery went well for your cousin, Starr, and your Auntie Rose. I figured why not me too?"

"But, Mama, Starr was only seventeen then, and today her health is horrible! In fact she was to participate in the pre-wedding activities today, but was so worn, she purposely stayed in Des Moines. Her doctor told her, either take it easy, or she would be back in the hospital, instead of being my maid of honor!" Lydia noticed their fingers were intertwined. "As for Auntie Rose—she had to lose, I don't know, about fifty pounds, *before* the doctor would even consent to surgery? She's a big woman again and forever reminds me, in her ever outspoken manner, she's my only aunt still alive!"

"Sounds like Rosie! She always had a mouth on her!" A smile etched across Frances' face. "Baby, it may not have been the right thing to do, but for me—it was what I wanted!"

Lydia's hand was squeezed tighter. It gave her strength. "Later on, when I was about nineteen or so, I was in Dr. Siege's office. He told me, he advised you against the surgery. He told me there was no reason for you to die. He told me that! Why didn't I stop you? I should have begged you!"

"Honey, there was no way you could! Your daddy tried, too. It was my choice to go ahead on."

"But why, Mama? Why? You knew people were against it! Why?" Lydia whispered.

"Looking back, it was my personal goal," Frances paused and turned away. "I dreamt of always being thin. I figured this was my last go at it. Unfortunately, it was my last go at everything."

"Don't you see? Size was not that big of a deal! My God! You could be here! With me!" Lydia heard the voice of a seven year old. Her voice. A stomped foot was the only missing element. Lydia was surprised she was still within her mother's grasp.

"Ah, still the only child, I see! Wanting everything your own way! I do wish Seth all the luck in the world!"

"The guy's got it good, and he knows it!" Lydia teased. She wanted the mood to lighten.

"Well, we shall see, won't we?"

"Mama, let's go on to something else, huh?"

"Baby, please let me—I need to finish. Please?"

Lydia sighed and nodded. *I don't want to hear these things, but I want you to stay with me.*

"Baby, in all seriousness, it was my time to go. It seems I always knew I wouldn't see you grow up. Remember, there was a morning, I drove you to school and I instructed you, in the event I should die, I must be buried in a blue dress, and holding a red rose?"

"Yea, Mama. what a great thing to lay on a kid, who's only goal, in life, was to color within the lines!"

Lydia heard her mother chuckle softly. Well, you got me there! Very bad timing on my part and I do apologize. Can you forgive me?"

"I'll try!" Lydia permitted a small smile. "When Daddy planned your funeral, I told him what you told me, and he already knew."

"Yes, baby, he did. Come on, let's sit down again. It'll be all right. I promise."

Lydia gave no resistance as she was motioned to sit on the bed. A cool breeze circled about the room. The plastic, covering her gown, rippled with its contact.

Her mother's touch gave Lydia power to continue. "You had the rose. The undertaker changed it everyday. Did you know Grace took me to funeral home to see you?"

"Yes, yes I did."

"I was so scared! And so sad. Grace was wonderful! We'd gone grocery shopping at Fareway. I'm sure it was just a ploy to get me out of the house. On the way out of Fareway, I asked Grace if we could walk over to the funeral home so I could see you. I think I was more petrified when she agreed! Looking back, I'm sure Grace wasn't sure what to expect. Whether or not I was going to go berserk or what. *I* didn't know what to expect!" Lydia wiped her forehead and licked her lips. "When I first saw you, lying there, it was like you were asleep. Then I remembered—and I nearly broke down. There were flowers everywhere! I was amazed—so many people knew who you were. Then I thought of Morgan and that she lost her mom when she was ten, and now we were both in the same boat."

"Baby, I am more sorry than you know, that—"

"Mama, now I need you to let me finish, or I never will get this all out. This stuff has been buried as long as you."

"I understand, Lydia. Please go on"

Lydia inhaled and continued, "People I never knew, including your brother Roland, showed up on our doorstep. My god, he sat at our kitchen table and wailed like a newborn! Actually more than I did. I wondered where was he when you were alive? That day seems both forever ago and then like yesterday. It all happened so fast! You were there one minute and gone the next! I mean, I was glad everybody remembered you, but I wanted them out of my house. I wanted a life back. It was only going to be daddy and me, but I wanted to get on with it. Do you understand?"

Frances nodded and Lydia's hand was squeezed harder. "Yes, my angel, I do."

"Well, after the— I mean, after *your* funeral, I thought it was finally over. I *needed* it to be over. I was so very wrong! After the graveside, everyone went to the Bethel Baptist Church and ate the food that had covered every inch of our kitchen. I had no clue this was procedure! Geesh, I certainly had no appetite! I wanted to wake up from this horrible dream! I wanted to be out riding bikes with Tilda. Not having Daddy ask me which headstone I thought was the nicest! I longed to get back to some normalcy. I practically counted down seconds till I could walk the halls of Brenner Junior High!"

"You did? Really? Well, you always seemed to enjoy school."

"Mama, I did like school, but after you died, it turned into more of my sanctuary. I was comfortable knowing what was going to happen, at least five out of the seven week days. Unlike, living without you."

"You had to live and learn. You were so young! Baby, I am so sorry—"

Lydia heard the sorrow. "Yes, I suppose it was. The entire episode exhausted me! To this day, I marvel how Daddy handled it! At the church he sat beside me, urging me to eat. All I wanted was some jello. Unfortunately, the only jello was green jello. On top of my world capsizing, green jello was not my idea of a life preserver!" Lydia surprised herself by laughing. It felt good and her heart seemed to resume its regular pace.

"I can only imagine. As I recall you favored strawberry jello, with sliced bananas, and whipped cream on top!"

"Y-you remember?"

"Of course, I do!" Frances beamed. "Baby, if it's not too difficult, I would really like to know more about that time."

Lydia swallowed hard. "Well, I hated your hair. It wasn't pretty like you always had it!"

Frances coughed. "It was pretty all right. *Pretty bad,* wasn't it?"

Lydia chuckled and nodded. It was obvious her mother was trying to suppress laughter.

"Really, in Emma Jean's defense, she was really torn up. There she was, suppose to work on a friend of hers. Nonetheless, though, I wanted to slap her silly. And I wanted to double slap my other sister, Mae for wanting you to change the dress you chose to wear to my funeral!"

"That dress! Oh, I was ticked at her too! You made that dress for me—and Mae thought it was just too bright! Well, at thirteen, I didn't feel black was much of a fashion statement! I wanted to wear something special and that dress was it. You made it for me, so that was my choice! Hey, the turquoise and flowers suited me just fine!"

"Ha! You definitely stood up for yourself! I was proud!"

Lydia grinned. "Everybody watched Daddy and me at the funeral home. Now, I'm sure everyone wondered what this guy was going to do with this teenage daughter! We sat so close to your casket, I could have touched it. I just wanted you to wake up and go home with us."

"Lydia, I did too. During those times, I saw most all that happened, especially when your daddy told you I was gone. I had to see you and be with you.. That look on your face—" Frances' voice lowered. "That look, I carry forever. You were devastated! I screamed to turn it all back!"

"Then why, Mama? Why? You were not the only one to die that morning. Two others did too. How could you not fathom that would happen?" Lydia got up and walked to her wedding dress. She touched a sleeve. It was as smooth as her mother's touch. "You left behind a husband and a thirteen year old daughter! What were you thinking? Nobody wanted you to have that surgery! Nobody! I think you were just plain selfish! You were being a selfish bitch!"

What am I doing? Oh, my lord, what did I just say? My Mama is here from Heaven and I call her a selfish bitch. Lydia covered her mouth. "Look, I don't know what happened. I don't know what to say— Oh, I am so sorry!"

"Lydia baby, it's ok. Trust me, you have the right to say anything to me."

"Yea, but what I said— I mean, I don't even cuss in front of Daddy!"

"Well, I'm not exactly thrilled, but you're too big to spank. Lydia, it is *your* right. You can say anything you want. But before we go any further, how about we get out of here for awhile?"

•◆•

"What?" Lydia hadn't contemplated going anywhere this time of night. Especially with someone who had not walked among the living in over twenty-five years! "You want to leave? And do what? Mama, I'd hadn't even thought of this! Do you realize how late it is?"

"How about a drive?"

Didn't she hear what I said? Lydia was dumbstruck. "A what?"

"A drive. Why not? It might be fun."

"*Might* is the key word, Mama!"

"I'd like to see how this ol' town of Brenner has changed!"

Lydia was surprised how her mother's demeanor had lightened. "Mama, it must be close to one or one thirty now! It's too late!'"

"Honestly, dear, it's closer to twelve-thirty. So, c'mon let's go. The fresh air should do us both good!"

"Twelve thirty? You mean all this has happened in only a half hour?"

Jangles jetted to life and scampered down the attic's steps, barking the entire way. Not a peep ebbed from her parents' bedroom. Why hadn't Jangles' barking roused them?

"What about clothes?" Lydia asked. "I don't think your heavenly robe or my flannel nightshirt is suitable riding gear. It's pretty chilly outside! Uh, I'll go change, I guess. And you really want to do this?" *She can't be serious!*

"Don't start doubts now, daughter." Frances commanded. "Go to your bedroom and look upon your bed. The dog and I will be waiting by the front door. Now go on."

Lydia was confused, but did as she was told. She somehow managed down the attic's steps and into her room. On her bed, were black sweatpants and a gold sweatshirt. *Iowa Hawkeye* colors! Her favorite black Reeboks, and black socks, rested beside them. No time to ask any questions. Lydia slid into the clothes and stepped from her room. She walked around the corner, and headed to the front door. Mama and Jangles were not there.

"Mama? Mama, where are you?" Lydia hissed. She didn't want to wake Daddy and Jewel and have to explain why she was calling out to a dead person. "Mama? Please, where are you?"

Just then Jangles appeared from her parents' bedroom. He looked up at her, turned and trotted back to their room. She followed him, afraid of what she might find. "Mama?"

"It's all right, baby. I'm in here."

Lydia peeked into the room. Daddy and Pearl both snored as the Andy Griffith show whistled from the television. Why was Mama in here? *She's so close to Daddy— Wonder if he wakes up?*

"You two would always watch this show together!"

"MAMA! What are you doing in here?".

"Hush, don't worry. I wanted to look at your father. He's been through so much. He still looks like that young man I met, so many years ago. He tried to be all that! Ha! What a sight! Hair, greased and slicked back, with his mighty bottle of Johnny Walker Red. He—"

"MOTHER!" Lydia loved the reminiscing, but she wanted to get out of there.

Lydia, with mouth gaped open, watched her mother's fingertips trace her father's forehead.

"Sleep well, my love. There should have been so much more. Perhaps another time." Then Frances bent and kissed his forehead.

How long had it been, since Lydia witnessed such a thing? Would Daddy even feel it? Were those tears in Mama's eyes?

"All right, Lydia, let's go."

As Frances walked past her, Lydia noticed her mother's outfit almost duplicated her own, except her sweatshirt had IOWA written across the chest in black. They resembled sisters. Not the mother and daughter, that they were. Jangles even donned a black sweater, with a yellow I on his back.

After Lydia secured his leash, the trio stepped into the October night. Lydia was unsure what to say and remained silent as they walked the few feet to her white car. She slid the key into the passenger side's door and turned .

Frances broke the silence. "I'd like to drive!"

"What? You? Drive? Mama, you've got to be joking! This is not 1971! Things have changed!" Lydia couldn't contain her laughter and hoped she didn't offend.

"Humph! Oh, come now! How hard is it to turn the key, put the car into drive, and foot the gas? Hmm? Has that all changed? I mean, are you driving a stick shift now?"

"Well, no—"

"Then, girl, open up this door, you get in, and give me the keys!"

"Mother! You can't be serious!" Yet, Lydia saw determination in her mother's eyes. Lydia opened the door, hit the electric lock button, and hesitantly handed over the keys, while Jangles held court in the back seat.

Lydia stared in disbelief as Frances situated herself behind the steering wheel. When she shut the door, Frances screamed as the seatbelt automatically crossed her torso. "Hey! They never did *that* before!"

Lydia laughed. "So things haven't changed, huh? Welcome to the nineties, Mama! Be careful, my baby has less than five thousand miles on it!"

"Yes, yes, five thousand miles. Yes, whatever you say! Now, let me get my barrings! I must say this car is very nice. What kind is it?"

"It's a Mitsubishi Diamante!" Lydia announced proudly, caressing the tan leather interior.

"A Mits-su Dee—a *what*?"

"A Mitsubishi Diamante, Mama. It's Japanese!" How funny and cute Mama looked with her eyes all big, Lydia thought. "My last car was too! That one was a black Nissan Maxima. I would have kept it too, but I wanted a sun roof! And I got a pretty good deal on my white diamond here."

"Sun roof? Japanese? You drive foreign cars? For glory sakes, Lydia! What's the matter with a good ol' Chevy? That's what we always had! Are you too snooty or something? We never taught you that!"

"Are you mad at me, Mama?"

"Lydia AnMarie Burscot!"

Uh, oh, Mama was using the whole name. Was asparagus far behind?

"For glory sakes, what are you doing in foreign cars? Nobody in their right mind —"

"Mama, things change! In fact, everybody in their right mind buys foreign!"

"Oh, no, well, I wouldn't! Give me a Chevy any day! None of this other country razzmatazz for this girl!"

With that declaration, Frances fired up the engine and shifted into drive.

Perhaps, things hadn't changed that much after all.

•◆•

"So Mama, where we headed?"

"Let's see, I'd like ice cream. Yes, that's the ticket—I want— ice cream! Out to the Tasty Treat it is."

"You've got to be kidding! TZ's closed for the night!"

"And you know he cleans that place up, spic and spac every night! And why are you so bent out of shape about things I suggest?"

"Mama, I don't know. I mean, this feels weird. And I certainly didn't plan on any socializing!"

"We'll just be there in a few minutes. Where's this spontaneity that you pride yourself on?"

"Huh? How did you know that? I—"

You had such a crush on him, didn't you?"

"Why did you cut me off?" Lydia met eyes with Frances, then returned her eyes to Third Street.

"Because *I'm* the Mama. Hey, I recollect your crush on him. You thought he was so cute, even though his bangs made him look like a sheepdog."

"Mother!"

'Oh he won't even remember me anyway, Lydia. Besides a taste of ice cream sounds mighty fine!"

"So no ice cream in Heaven, eh, Frances?"

Frances playfully lifted an eye brow and whistled. "That's mother, mom, or some variation there of! You will never be big enough to call me by my first name! Got that girl?"

Lydia smirked. "Gotcha"

From Third Street, Frances turned left onto Willis Avenue. Except for one lone set of headlights, passing them on the opposite side, the glaring lampposts were their only companions.

"I can't believe we're doing this! You, me and the hound!" Lydia suddenly felt queasy.

"What do you mean, baby?"

"Well, one minute you're in Heaven, well, I'm *assuming* you're from Heaven!"

"I beg your pardon, missy?"

Lydia spit out giggles. This was too good! She finally got one over the queen.

"Hmm, trying to be funny aren't we? Yes, just as funny as the year you slit open them Christmas presents!"

"Uh—"

"Uh, my be-*hind*! Now, what was it you were attempting to say?"

Lydia's cheeks flushed as her mother gleamed. This wasn't going to be as easy as she thought. Time hadn't exactly soften everything!

"Uh, what I meant was—here we are, and we're going for ice cream. Not exactly a Ten Commandments kind of moment!"

"That movie scared you."

"Mother please! Not the whole movie, just the burning bush part. Geesh! Don't you ever let up?

"Let up what, dear?"

"Ugh And you're getting off the subject!" Lydia heaved an exasperated sigh. Now she realized what her own friends went through with her—when, during conversations, she took off on other tangents. This was a delicious irony.

"You were on my lap and pretended to be asleep."

"Uh, well, I was—"

"Yes, dear, sure thing. You always seem to be awake when Moses parted the Red Sea, though!"

"Oh, *whatever*, mother!" Lydia faked a yawn as she heard her mother laugh. Lydia glanced at the speedometer. At least Mama adhered to the speed limit. She could have a heavy foot and all they needed was to get stopped, by one of Brenner's eight finest, in the middle of the night, because her *dead* mother was speeding.

Their arrival time at the Tasty Treat was an estimated fifteen more minutes. Even though Ms. Timex was not with her, Lydia knew exactly the length of time it took. Some habits were hard to break, even after twenty years! She sighed, and relaxed against the head rest.

"Mother? Mama. Just feels weird to say it."

"Well, it feels wonderful to hear! You never called Jewel that. Why? You two grew close over the years."

Lydia gazed out the window. "I don't know. There were times I wanted to. Ya know? But it just wasn't the same. No disrespect to her. Just wasn't the same! I mean, you were my one and only mother." Tears came back and the back of her hand became a kleenex. "Look, Mama, I've always wanted to know something. Would you promise to answer?"

"Why, yes, baby, of course!"

Lydia saw a familiar line of concern between her mother's eyebrows. "I've always wanted to know, just what did you want me to be when I grew up? You thought about it, I know!" Lydia tensed up, she was almost was afraid of the answer.

"Well, first, I wanted you to be happy. I always intended you to head to college right after high school. That fell like a ton of bricks."

Lydia's skin prickled. The subject of college was difficult, even now, when she actually was going to the university. "Mama, I tried!"

"No, you did not! Oh, you tried on the *happy* all right, but the college part—huh! You needed help—guidance!" Frances curtly accentuated every word. "You applied only to the University of Iowa. They even told you to enroll at a community college, to get your grades up, then transfer. You didn't. You gave up!"

Yep, this was Mama all right and Lydia had to make her listen. "I did not give up! How dare you say that! I went to that travel school in Florida."

"Yes, Lydia you did. And you got a straight 'A' in making long distance phone calls to TZ and charging them to your dad."

Lydia was flabbergasted. No words inched their way from her open mouth.

"Uh-huh. I can see you have alot to say." Frances taunted. "Now, truthfully, I am proud you didn't experiment with cocaine or any other kind of drug. They were there for the taking!"

"You know that? Geesh, is nothing a secret to you?"

Frances waved her off. "You needed more guidance. Dee was confident you knew the difference between right and wrong. To travel the correct path. But you were very impatient. He didn't realize he needed to give some input. No matter how mature you were or he *thought* you were—a helping hand was needed. Your daddy was so unsure of what exactly to do."

"Daddy tried to—"

"Daddy tried, but he did not *do*! Your dad is strong and silent. Sometimes the right things just weren't spoken! He loves you so much! There he was, left alone, with a teenage daughter and such responsibility." Frances' voice softened. "Donald Burscot did his best. You were and still are his world. If you had decided to live in Arizona, with Mae and your cousins, you'd be praying for both of us to be at your wedding!"

Lydia's eyes widened. "Really?

"Yes, really. Do have any idea what pressure others put on your daddy?"

"I-I never really thought about it! Isn't that awful? I mean, I never saw Daddy cry. Not even once!" Lydia felt so ashamed. To this day, she only really had thought about her own pain. Not giving too much to the depth of pain Daddy suffered. Maybe because, he always appeared so strong. So silent. How could she have been so selfish?

"Lord have mercy on me! How could I have been so out of it? I remember, there was a night, Daddy asked me if I wanted to go somewhere and 'have fun' all the time. I could not imagine! That night, I tried to cook us a chicken dinner. I wanted so badly to copy you. Right done to the dollop of sugar on the kernel corn! After he asked me, I just figured he didn't want me anymore. I was devastated! It hurt so much!" Even now, the memory saddened her. "He reassured me he still wanted me and never brought it up again. Not until my eighteenth birthday party. Now *that* was a night!" Lydia giggled. "Both Daddy and

Jewel were shocked so many kids showed up at our little house. So much fun! Daddy told the kids he would have been lost without me."

"He spoke the truth, Lydia. Doubts ran rampant within him too. Think about it, there he was, with a teenage daughter on the verge of being a young woman, while he was a man, far from old. Difficult indeed. He did what he thought was right. It killed him to ask, but he had to find out. He felt pressured. Mae thought it would be best for you to be around your cousins."Lydia sighed. "Now the best thing Mae could have done, was to have never left Des Moines! Then Starr and Willace would have still been close. Unfortunately, that was not the case. Also, after you died, Mae really kept her distance. Granted Arizona was a long way—"

"Honey, like I said Mae thought it was the right thing. Starr and you were just like sisters."

Mama was right. Things just didn't happen like they were suppose to. "Was Daddy scared I might say I wanted to go? I almost said yes, because I thought that's what he wanted. I never wanted to leave him. I just wonder if he thought I did."

"Lydia, in the back of your daddy's mind, he thought you would leave him forever! He sweat bullets, working up his nerve to ask you! That man was so twisted inside. Do *you* understand?"

Lydia dropped her head and nodded. Oh how could she not think what Daddy was up against? How could she not see? Most of the time, Daddy held himself up. There were down times too, one time in particular—

Early November, not quite two months after Mama left, Daddy was late from work. It was nearly five, and he was never this late. Lydia watched an unfamiliar car steer into their drive way. Who was it?

Daddy was no where in sight. Wait! Lydia saw him spring up in the backseat. What was going on?

A man stepped from the driver's side, and opened the back door. Lydia saw the man bend into the back seat and seemed to pull Daddy out of the car. Daddy had on his favorite navy blue trench coat. Why did he have it on this time of day? Lydia's stomach flip flopped. Daddy bobbed and weaved his way to the front step.

Lydia tried to be funny and teased him about being drunk, as he stumbled past her. Her blood boiled and her head pounded. She glanced at the unfamiliar car. The man still stood by the open door. A woman now stood on the passenger side of the car. She looked sad. *Not as sad as I feel,* Lydia thought *Would they take her with them?*

Daddy struggled to the couch and plopped face down. Somehow he mumbled for Lydia to hurry and get the bucket. She trembled as she ran to the bathroom to get the green plastic bucket. Only it was too late. The curdling sounds of Daddy throwing up punished her ears. She wanted to do the same.

She had to flee. Lydia dropped the plastic bucket and raced to her room. She still had on her skirt and heels from school—she didn't care! There was no time to change! She had to get out. Lydia threw on her brown CPO jacket, and headed for their home's back door.

Earlier, Tilda had canceled their trip for downtown. There was just too much homework to do. At the time, that was ok. Now, was totally different. Lydia slid her phone from its hook. *Wonder if Daddy was somehow able to answer it? He would surely embarrass her more.*

Lydia ran from the house and crossed Seventh Street. She turned the corner at the Bethel Baptist Church. A ledge set a few feet from her. The very same ledge where, when she was small, Daddy held her hand, for balance, as she walked on its top. On this day, she sat and cried.

Somehow Lydia managed to dry her tears and strolled downtown. She waved and smiled to kids she knew. *No one must see how sad she was.* Lydia walked through Spurgeons and then Anthony's, and purchased nothing. They didn't sell mommies at either store.

Darkness was starting. Lydia knew she had to get home. Even with Daddy drunk, he might be worried about her. Lydia walked slowly up Rawson Street, then again turned the corner at

Bethel Baptist Church, onto Seventh Street. Lydia eased into the house, the same way she left, through the back door.

She heard nothing, except Daddy's snoring. Lydia closed her bedroom's door and tried, quietly, to put her phone back on its hook. She situated herself at her desk, attempting to do home-work. Minglee found her lap and settled in. Lydia felt more guilty, because she left her kitty all alone. Wonder if he had been scared?

Almost immediately, the phone rang. Lydia grabbed for it on the first ring. Of course, it was Tilda wondering what happened. Lydia tried to laugh it all off by telling her Minglee knocked it off the hook, and she just now discovered it. Lydia envied Tilda because she had both her parents.

Lydia heard a knock on the door. Daddy. She shivered in her chair. Her back remained to him. His steps grew closer. Lydia felt the cold press of his face against her right cheek. She refused to turn. The stench of alcohol mixed with vomit slapped her.

"Baby, are you mad at Daddy?"

The smell was unbearable. "Yes." Lydia whispered. She still could not turn to face him.

"Do you still love Daddy?"

Lydia gulped. She wanted to cry. But she wouldn't. She wouldn't let him see her be sad. "You're still my daddy." Lydia placed her hand under his chin, still not looking at him.

He kissed her cheek and left her room.

Lydia soon heard the television blare from the living room. And then she cried.

• ◆ •

As if her thoughts were heard, Lydia felt her left leg being squeezed.

"Baby, he struggled so much. He wanted to give you every-thing. Your father never wanted to fail you. But parents make mistakes too. Please, never doubt his devotion to you."

"I know. I know. But sometimes it was hard!" Lydia muffled. "As time passed, I realized I was luckier with one parent than some of my friends were with two."

"See, you're using that gray matter God gave you. During some moments, you forgot about your greatest gift! The beauty is, you're using it now. You've always possessed the ability to evolve. Now, to what I wanted for your life—I wanted you to be whatever you wanted to be. I wanted you to be happy."

"That's the answer I'm going to get? That's it? Come on, Mama, I somehow doubt it! Can't you be a bit more specific?" Lydia couldn't hide her frustration. As outspoken as Lydia remembered Mama to be, this was not good enough.

Lydia watched Frances lick her lips. "Ok, baby why don't you tell me what you aspired to be. I am curious!"

"Mama, come on! I asked you! Why so secretive?" Why are you doing this? It's an easy question!"

"Lydia, please, baby. I've always wanted to know."

"Oh all right!" Lydia heaved. "But you really have no clue, do you?" She watched her mother shake her head. Lydia was puzzled. How could Mama not know? Lydia turned away, in time to watch Brenner Junior High whiz past. "I wanted to dance."

"What did you say, Lydia?"

Lydia returned her attention to her mother. "I wanted to be a dancer, Mama. I wanted to dance. In particular, ballet."

"Ballet? I never thought—I mean, I wasn't even sure you *liked* the lessons to begin with."

Lydia heard genuine surprise. "You're right Mama, I hated the lessons. I *liked* the final result!" *I have to let you know how it really was—*

"You never said anything to—"

Lydia cut her off. "Seeing the junior high building, made me remember another time and place. When I was four years old, we walked up to the junior high. You took me to my first ever dance recital. I didn't have any idea what it was!"

"You were excited though. I must have said the right thing! I just had no idea!"

"Well, all I remember was a girl, in a blue frilly tutu , with blue toe shoes to match! I thought she was the most magnificent creature I'd ever seen!"

"Really? For glory's sake, your daddy and I never knew!"

"Oh, Mama, most definitely! I knew then I wanted to dance! That fall, you started me on lessons. They were okay, but I just wanted to be on my toes! I was only four, but I knew what I wanted! I guess, I was a little impatient!"

"Hmm—yes, even then!"

"Mama! Please, let me finish!" Lydia wanted to nip the sarcasm in the bud. "Then, at the next year's recital, one of the teacher's assistants, Jane Rae—remember her?" Lydia saw Frances nod. "She performed something from Swan Lake. She was the white swan that died. She was so pretty and on her toes!" Lydia heard her voice quicken.

"Lydia, I just had no idea. Why didn't you ever mention it? I'm sure if Madame Harris had known—"

Lydia cut her off again. "Oh, Mama, don't you remember? She said I looked like a perfect Hawaiian girl, and put me in that pink, fake grass skirt!"

"Well, baby, you were excited wearing that hula skirt! And as I recall you performed on a local television show, because of that very particular style of dance!"

"*Mother*, what kid wouldn't be excited about wearing that skirt? It glowed in the *dark*, for goodness sakes! And as for that show, our reward for being a 'talent sprout' was the passes to McDonald's!"

Both women laughed.

"Seriously, Lydia, why didn't you say something?"

"I just *knew* Madame Harris would put me on pointe shoes. All my friends were going on pointe, so I figured my time was coming!" Lydia heaved a sigh. "That year, I lost a lot of weight, and I figured that cinched the deal. Madame Harris was so happy for me! She showered me with so many compliments. So I just knew. *Just knew*!" Lydia slammed a fist on her thigh. She bit her bottom lip. "In all honestly, you're the one that busted my dreams, Mama!"

"Huh? What in heaven's name do you mean, Lydia? I can't imagine! I loved watching you dance!"

"There was a day, you told me black girls didn't have the right shape, like white girls, to be ballerinas. I wanted to cry."

"Did I say *that*? No, I couldn't have! Oh, my goodness!" Lydia watched the lightbulb go off in her mother's head. "I had no idea! Baby, I am so sorry! I was wrong in telling you that! I preached that you could be whatever you wanted to be. Yet, I went against my own words! It was my fault not to question when I was told. Madame Harris had plans for you, performing around the area. I was so excited, but you didn't seem anxious about the prospects!"

"I know Madame Harris had plans. But it was doing the hula. Honestly, Mama, I didn't see the appeal."

"But baby, you were so good."

"Yea, but it was the hula. I really couldn't fathom the thought of forming the moon with my hands, and Shriners applauding."

"I failed you on this, baby. Oh, I wish I would have known! Once again, I am so sorry!"

"Well, after that, the major thrill of dance did a *pas de deux* right out the window. All I wanted to do was dance on my toes! And ya know, after all of these years, part of me still does! We were driving over the train tracks, on Seventh Street, when you lowered the boom!" Lydia suddenly felt awkward and silly. No one knew about her dreams—until now.

"By goodness, Lydia, how do you remember the exact moment?"

"Mama, everyone remembers when their hearts break." Lydia shrugged her shoulders. "Look, we're almost to the Tasty Treat—but you have time to tell me what you *really* wanted for me."

Lydia heard her mother inhale deeply. "Baby, in all honestly, what I wanted for you, were the dreams I had for myself."

So my intuition was right.

"I think you knew, at a young age, I sometimes seemed to nudge you in other directions. Directions, you particularly didn't care for, but where I wanted to go. That was wrong, and I apologize." Lydia's left leg was being squeezed. "I wanted to be a nurse, and never was, so I figured, why not you? You talked about taking French in high school. I couldn't understand why. The look on your face—I think I may have even laughed that day."

"You did."

Lydia watched Frances bite her bottom lip. "Oh, I really hurt you that day. Ranks right up there for not knowing you wanted to be a ballerina, huh? That was wrong of me. Maybe, in a way, I was jealous. You had more choices than I ever did. Or I was angry you didn't share my dreams."

"French is what Tilda talked me into. It sounded so cool. Truth be known, Mama, I enjoyed it! Everything could not be for you!" Lydia snapped. "And, you're right, I noticed your pushing. Over time, if you had chosen to live, I eventually would have learned to fight you and our fights would have been monumental. I was too young back then. It was just easier to keep quiet."

"But imagine where you would be now—"

"Mama, that's all I can do—*imagine*."

• ◆ •

Frances steered into the Tasty Treat and parked beside TZ's black Blazer. Lydia noticed most of the lights were shut off. Yet, there was enough light that Lydia caught a glimpse of TZ's shadow.

"Ok, we're here," announced Frances, as she cut the engine.

"Now, what, Mama? I just can't go up to TZ and say, 'Oh, hi, Hon! Hey, I know it's the middle of the night, but gee, my mother, the ghost, and I would love a delicious frozen dairy confection!' No, ma, ain't gonna happen!" She rolled her eyes to make her point.

She watched Frances lift an eyebrow, and then laugh. "No, I don't believe that would be too cool. Tell him you're doing one last spin through town, before tying the knot. You just wanted to see him and I'm just a friend. Lydia, you know TZ won't have a clue who I am! There is absolutely nothing to worry about! Come on, let's get out!"

"Hey, I'm not introducing you! Not no way, not no how! You are out of your dead mind! OK, I'll just walk up to the back door and—"

"Rita! Whatta ya doin' here? Hey, ain't you supposed to be asleep, dreaming, of this grand weddin' of yours?"

Lydia snapped her head around and met TZ's face, level with hers. His breath rinsed her face. Hadn't she kept the window rolled up? The night air was chilly—so the window was all the way up. Wasn't it? She must have hit the button—by accident—to lower it. Yes, that must have been it! She shook the surprise from her eyes by blinking twice. "Uh, we came out for some ice cream."

"Hey, you know the hours! Just 'cause you're gettin' married tomorrow, you think you can get anything! Think again, babe! And how in the world are you lettin' somebody else drive this fancy car of yours? You practically charge me just to look at it! Hey, but that time I tried to teach you how to drive a stick, by practicing on my truck, and then the transmission went out!" a sheepish grin crossed TZ's face.

"Oh, come on, TZ! You said it wasn't my fault. Anyway, we want one of those delicious chocolate covered vanilla bars with the peanuts. The ones you freeze in the Dixie cups! Ah, come on—just for us!" Lydia winked, which made his grin spread more. This guy would always be special to her!

"Well, I dunno!" TZ peeked into the back seat. "Hey, looks like ya brought the dog too! How did Jewel let him outta the house?"

"Oh, she was sleeping and he wasn't, so we brought him with us!" Frances replied.

Lydia knew color drained from her face as Frances spoke. *How dare she say something?*

TZ looked past Lydia and eyed Frances up and down. Lydia wondered how could this be happening. TZ was a bigger flirt than she was, and he was about to hit on her *mother*! *Her dead mother.* A shot of schnapps would do nicely, at the moment. Lydia had to say something. Anything would do!

"Lydia, aren't you going to introduce us?" asked Frances. "And why don't we get out and stretch our legs?"

"Huh? Yea, ok. Out the car." *I sound like a bumbling idiot!*

TZ opened the door for her. Frances made her way around to the passenger side. TZ did a double take on their almost matching outfits. "Hey, you two girls are practically twins."

If you only knew.

"Looks good! I have two of the prettiest Iowa Cheerleaders in my mist!"

Why is she giggling like some high school girl? And where is that schnapps?

"So Rita, what's your friend's name?"

Now the moment of truth dawned. Lydia swallowed a deep breath and prayed for the best. "This is, er, um—this is Frances—*Franny.*"

Frances flashed a smile. For some reason, it reassured Lydia. Maybe this wouldn't be so bad after all. Then Frances took the smile to TZ's direction. "Well, I've known our little Lydia for quite awhile. We've been out of touch, and just so happened, we recently ran into each other. So this sweet little girl extended an invite for tomorrow's festivities!"

Yea, the cemetery. Quite a happy hour rendezvous spot.

"Now, TZ, what does that stand for? And why do you call her Rita?

"Hee, hee," TZ chortled.

Lydia noticed how TZ loved the attention from this new woman. A woman, who just happened to be, her mother. A woman whose most recent address, up till a few moments ago, was Rural Route Heaven. Lydia pictured her own body, to be a stick of dynamite—set to explode—soon.

"Well, TZ stands for Theodore Zacahriah. My folks were into some heavy duty names when I popped out. Hee hee. I've been TZ since grade school. Man, it was simpler for me to say. As for Rita, well, hee, hee, that's been since high school. I looked at her, one day in the hall way, and said she looked like a Rita! She was ticked for awhile, but got over it. So she's been that ever since. Huh, Rita?"

"Yes, he's right. On top of that he always wanted my sour apple bubble gum!" Lydia chimed. "The big lug would just snatch it! Without even bothering to ask!"

"Oh, yea, you fought, all right—but you always gave in! You were so crazy about me!"

"It was more like you were and still *are* crazy! But hey, I was young, so I didn't know better!"

"Rita!" TZ's pretended exasperation made laughter ring. TZ quieted himself, and continued, "OK, tell you both what I'm gonna do. Since I've had the pleasure of meeting you, Franny, and with Rita gettin' married tomorrow—I'll give ya some bars for the road. Just bring back my cooler, ok, Rita?

Lydia nodded.

"I'll give you ladies three apiece. That oughta hold you till you come out here after you say them vows of yers. 'cause that stuff you catered, won't be half as good!"

"Uh, TZ?" Lydia sighed loudly, "The ice cream, ya know, for the reception? It's coming from the Tasty Treat, remember?"

"Oh, yea? Hee Hee! I forgot. Gee, hope I've made it! Oh, say, you paid for it yet?"

Lydia raised an eyebrow, while Frances continued chuckling.

"Oh, ok, let me go get them bars. Just take me a minute. Be right back."

With that, Frances and Lydia watched TZ walk into the Tasty Treat. "You really liked him, didn't you?"

"Yep, he was special all right. Their paths just didn't cross. Or they just didn't cross enough. He always said he loved me. I never doubted him. Just a nice girlhood thing."

A few minutes passed, then the screen door flew open. TZ walked out with a red, white, and blue styrofoam cooler. "I'm such a nice guy, I put a dozen of em in here. Your dad and Jewel may want some."

"Hon-NEE, put that there cooler right in here!" Frances ordered as she opened the front door. TZ did as he was told and slid the cooler to the middle.

"Man oh man! I'll definitely have a sugar buzz because of this and I can think of no better reason! Thanks a lot, TZ! I'm sure they'll like a few too!" Lydia pecked TZ's cheek. "We're going to get on our way. Thanks so much again, honey!"

"Ahh—she still does love me! Maybe I better call up that ol' stupid Seth!"

"Oh hush with you! Come on, uh, Franny—we need to go!"

"Ha! Yes, TZ, it was a pleasure meeting you! And I want to say thanks for the bars too!" Frances stuck out her hand to shake.

Instead TZ took her hand and kissed it. "Pleasure meeting you too, Franny. And Rita, you know it's always a pleasure. You two be careful. And I'll see you tomorrow!" TZ shut Lydia's door and stood as they backed out of his shop's parking lot. Frances honked as they surged forward. TZ waved and then disappeared into the Tasty Treat.

"Ok, Mama, want a bar? Can you handle it?"

"Can I handle? Can I handle *what*? Baby, you know your mama can eat and drive with the best of them! You better unwrap me one of them bars!"

Lydia unwrapped a bar and handed it to her. Frances seemed to savor the bite. "How's it taste?"

"After all this time, it tastes fantastic! I'm glad he gave us more!"

"Well, I'm glad! I guess you don't have much ice cream in Heaven, huh?"

"Something like that!" Frances replied with a smile.

Lydia unwrapped her own bar and settled in the seat. "Where to now, Mama?"

"I'd love to head to Des Moines. One of those Millie's tenderloins would be great! And to go along with this ice cream! Hmm-mmm-mmm."

"Then why don't we?"

"Wouldn't it be fun? Going to Des Moines again, like we did in the old days? But, baby, I want us to have some peace and quiet, so we can talk."

"Oh, ok. Back to house then?"

"No, somewhere else. Hmm—is Davis Park still around?"

"Sure is. You want to go there?"

"Yes, it would be nice to see it again. When you were little, you gathered Easter eggs there, splashed in the baby pool, and tried to roller skate." Frances mused. "Well, you were good at the splashing part, anyway!"

"Gee, thanks Mama!" Lydia deadpanned.

"Just kidding, Thomasina! Just kidding!" Frances took another bite of her ice cream bar.

Lydia suggested they forget about driving down Willis and take the Brenner's bypass. "I want you to see how this town has changed in thirty years. Also it'll make the trip quicker."

The speed limit was now fifty-five, yet Lydia had to occasionally remind Frances of that. Somewhere between cruising up Willis and getting onto the 141 Bypass, she'd found her lead foot.

Lydia was amazed how her mother could begin her second bar, while Lydia wasn't near done with her first. Ice cream must really be in short supply. "So, Mama," Lydia began, trying to swallow ice cream, "How does Brenner look?"

"Well, back then, this part of town, was a field for all the eye to see." Frances bit into her bar. "Now look."

Their path took them past Hy-Vee, one of the two grocery stores in town. In fact, it was brand, spanking new.

"Who would have thought Brenner would need such a big store! Things just keep growing!"

Yea, like me. And you missed it.

"Boy, look over there!" Frances pointed towards a sign, where a spot light shone on it.

The sign declared Brenner 'the place to be.' Next to the sign was a bright, all night gas station. Across the street, from them both, stood a dark McDonald's.

"I just can't believe this! None of this was here back then. None of it! Not even pavement! Train tracks crossed here. Nothing but a gravel road! You and Tilda rode bikes out to that cemetery pond, down that way." Frances gestured her head to the left. "It had to be three or four miles. And you nuts pedaled there! Ha! Ha! I'm impressed! Now, there was one Saturday morning you two planned to go and it began sprinkling. But it stopped enough, you two thought. It had to be about seven-thirty or so. You waited for Tilda on the Bethel Baptist Church steps, didn't you?"

Lydia didn't want to look. Her attention remained on her ice cream bar.

Frances continued, "Yes, you waited for Tilda, in the gentle rain. Your dad had gone out the night before and was asleep in a living room chair. You didn't want to stay. You didn't want Tilda to see him. I understand that. By the time you and Tilda made it home, the two of you were drenched! The rain spilled heavily that day and neither one of you cared! Just another adventure in your book. Just another escape. By the time you got home, you father was up and doing laundry and nothing was said."

Lydia cleared her throat. "You saw a lot, huh? During those times, I longed for you, more. Those times were so hard! I didn't have a solitary clue how to handle them. I just had to get out! Daddy didn't go out much—but enough. Even though I under-stand more now, it still hurts Counseling would have been great for us. Unfortunately, it was a time where you just didn't talk about such things. Our loss." Lydia lowered her head, suddenly feeling ashamed.

"True, both of you needed guidance, But you made it through. You should be proud."

"If you say so. But if you hadn't left, we—"

"Looks like we're here!" Frances cut in. "I'm going to park by the tennis courts, ok?"

•◆•

Frances steered the car into a parking space, and shut off the engine. Lydia rolled the window, halfway down. She heard the faint chirps of crickets. Shouldn't those ugly creatures be gone by now? It was October, for goodness sake! Lydia watched Frances finish her second ice cream bar. A street lamp gave Lydia enough light for another examination of her mother's face.

In all actuality, Mama was just three years older. Now, if she had lived, her age would be heading toward its seventieth year. Tonight, though Frances Marie Burscot was as young, vibrant and lovely as Lydia remembered. So young to die.

Mama's eyes were charcoal black and her complexion was lighter than Lydia's. Lydia had the mixture of Mama's orange coloring and Daddy's real dark skin. The lamppost's light caught the frost of Mama's glossed, perfectly rounded nails just right. There must be emery boards in Heaven, just no ice cream, Lydia reasoned.

Lydia situated herself and shut her eyes. She basked in the clean, sweetened air. It reminded her of that forgotten fragrance. "Mama, what was your favorite cologne? You wore—what was the brand? Wait! It was Faberge, wasn't it? It seemed like you had them all!" Lydia, with closed eyes, let the fragrance intertwine and brighten her memories.

"You're right. Faberge was my favorite brand. For my favorite—that's a hard question! Two that I really enjoyed, were Kiku and Tigress. But my all time favorite had to be Straw Hat!"

"That's it! Straw Hat! That's what you have on right now, isn't it?" Lydia happily exclaimed.

"Yes, I do. It's light. It reminds me of the first new days of Summer. The cologne and powder were packaged in a mini straw hat! You bought it, for me at Walgreens!"

"Ha! Ha! I sure did! I felt so grown up buying things for you both! I'd get Brut for Daddy. I'm sure the cost was nothing back then, but it was something to me!" Lydia opened her eyes and smiled.

"Speaking of gifts—do you also remember the day you slit open the Christmas packages?" Frances licked the last remnants of her third ice cream bar and glared at Lydia.

Lydia gulped. "Why are you bringing that up? I thought we covered that. And that day I had a cold."

"Uh-huh. A cold. Right, daughter. As I recall, that afternoon I headed to work. You were alone— for what? Three or four hours, till your daddy got home? But, oh no! You had to be Miss Nosy Butt. Just had to be! When I saw those packages, with that shabby tape job you did, Ooh, I almost went to Webster School and yanked your nosy butt out of there! What were you thinking?"

Why is Mama still mad at me, after all this time? Why is her voice getting louder? Is Mama gonna slap my hands?

"That somewhere, before then and Christmas, those packages weren't going to be handled? How did you expect them to get under the tree? Walk on their own?" Frances glanced out of the window, then returned her glare to Lydia. "Especially since they were on one side of the room and the tree was on the other? What were you thinking? I threatened to give them to the retarded kids I worked with. You were that close to having nothing, kiddo! It was *that* close." Frances positioned her thumb and index finger an inch or so apart.

"On Christmas morning, you got after me, each time I opened a gift. You kept telling me why should I open it since I already knew what was in it. I felt so stupid!"

"You should have! Did I ever spank you for that?"

"No, you didn't. The tone in your voice scared me enough."

"Well, since I didn't, then take this!" France smacked Lydia on the back of the head.

"Hey, what was that for?" Lydia asked as she rubbed the tender spot.

"Ah, I feel ever so much better now! Let's get out of the car and walk this ice cream off!"

Mama sounded so triumphant. Maybe it was finally physically punishing her for that Christmas, or the fact she had devoured three ice cream bars and had a major big time sugar buzz. If there were such things in Heaven.

Lydia peeked at Jangles, still snoring in the back seat. "Guess he'll be ok."

Both women exited the car, and stood side by side at its hood. A chill ran through Lydia as their shoulders touched. Wordless, with hands laced together, they walked into the darkness of Davis Park.

Questions, which needed answers, popped into Lydia's. "Mama, does it bother you Daddy being with Jewel? I mean, all these years? You two were together a long time, and the way you looked at him tonight." Lydia heard her mother sigh, then sigh again. No words came. "Mama, did I say something wrong? Have I overstepped some boundaries? Should I have left well enough alone? Mama?"

By Lydia's estimation, an eternity passed before her mother opened her mouth. "Baby, Jewel is good for your dad. She was good for you. Why didn't you give her more of a chance in the beginning?"

Lydia ran her fingers through her hair. This was stuff she didn't feel comfortable discussing with anyone. Especially her own long gone mother. Lydia tried to rid her throat of the ever growing frog. "Sure, Jewel was cool. But I was jealous and scared. Honestly, I did like her, but I resented her, because Daddy never told me she was moving in. In fact, I'm still waiting!" Lydia held her mother's hand tighter. "It was an afternoon, during our lunch hour, Loree, Tilda, and I were at our house, listening to records. We had just started our senior year and we were so giddy! Tilda spotted Jewel first. She screamed and said it looked like Jewel had a carload of stuff. Like she was moving in. I about passed out. All of us got quiet and the second Jewel stepped into the house, we hightailed it out! I was traumatized! I couldn't believe it! I had no idea, Jewel and Daddy were so tight! I was scared to come home after school. I just had no clue."

"Oh, come on, Lydia, you must have had *some* idea."

Lydia felt pressured, beyond her control. She swallowed. "They were seeing each other quite a bit. I knew that. Yet, Daddy never said a word about anything. Like how deep it was. But then of course, I never asked either. We both were at fault. My mind just focused on the fact, when Daddy spent the weekend in Des Moines, it was party time at the Burscot house!" That announcement made Lydia snicker.

"And you and your band of rogues came down, to this very Davis Park, and dumped your empty Pabst Blue Ribbon beer cans on Sunday mornings!" shot Frances.

"My goodness! What else do you know? On second thought, I don't even want to know!" Lydia said, as Frances playfully nudged against her. "But truthfully, if it weren't for Jewel's organization, my wedding plans wouldn't have materialized. She did everything on this end, down to getting Reverend Terry to officiate. I am truly blessed."

"Ahh, Reverend Terry. He was the first and only clergy person you knew so well. The first one that wasn't as old as Moses anyway. And you slow danced with him yet! You were so nervous. You didn't know what to do! You thought you were dancing with God! Well, I got news for you, deary."

"Mama!"

By now Frances laughed loudly. "And your friend, uh Jeannie, right?" Frances gave no time for an answer. "Well, she thought lightening would strike her for being guilty by association! That just tickles me! Why did it bother you so much? Revered Terry is still a man, honey."

"Yes, I know that! He just pledged his life to God and that little collar deal gave me the creeps, that's all!" Lydia tried to shake down her embarrassment. Useless.

"Whatever you say, Lydia AnMarie. Believe what you want." Frances tried to suppress her own laughter, yet snippets escaped "Come on, let's walk over to that bridge. And let's get back to the original subject, ok?"

"Yes, let's do. Even I get tired of hearing about myself."

"Sure, dear, what ever you say."

Lydia groaned.

"First of all, I'm glad things worked out between you and Jewel. And secondly, yes, I do miss your dad. We didn't have a chance to grow old together." Frances slowed her pace. "We had some pretty rough times too. More than once I thought about leaving. Then I regained my senses and worked things out."

"Unfortunately, Mama, you didn't regain your senses—the one time, it mattered most!"

"Lydia, I—"

•◆•

"We're here. The bridge awaits us." Lydia released Frances' hand and walked ahead. Lydia stopped in the bridge's center. It was no wider than a sidewalk and arched over a small creek. Lydia's memory traveled back to a time when she, Starr, and Willace, looked over this same bridge, scanning for tadpoles. Eventually, they waded into the clear, shallow water for a closer look. None of them were teenagers yet. Centuries ago.

Frances drew beside Lydia, and rested her arms on top of the iron railing. Lydia inspected her mother's profile again. It shimmered in the moonlight. Her skin appeared to be smooth as silk. That scent—that scent, of Straw Hat, laced the air.

Lydia returned her gaze to the creek. Moonbeams danced on the creek's top. The water's slow rush met her ears. It brought her comfort. Keeping her eyes on the creek, Lydia asked, "Mama, what about the men in my life? What did you think about them? You had opinions, I'm sure. I mean, how could I possibly find such a troop of swell winners, or for a more realistic term, idiots!"

"Ah, the men. Now, now, daughter, some weren't all that bad. There was some tough terrain. You were on the verge of being a young woman."

"Grace, Mary, and especially my cousin, Carol, helped me with those female things!" For some reason, Lydia needed to make it clear, she wasn't totally alone. Even though, she sometimes felt that way.

"Oh, honey, I know you did. They would have done anything for you. Yet, it really wasn't the same."

Lydia instinctively turned to face her mother, and found their eyes inspecting each other, then lowered her head. "You're right, it wasn't. I didn't have you for a long time, yet you taught me alot. Afterall, my friends thought you were the coolest mom! You filled me in about my period and boys, long before their moms did or if their moms ever did!"

"Ha, Ha. Well, I'm glad about that! There were things you needed to know. You discovered many more things by error. Some pain didn't have to happen."

Lydia covered her mother's hands, with her own. "Those errors toughened me up. But, what did you think about the men? I really want to know."

"Well, your father and I taught you to be open minded. And you most definitely are that! I didn't agree with all your choices, but I respected them. I never thought your open mind would include a man dressing in women's clothing, though!"

Lydia laughed, "Well, it just happened!"

"But then who am I too say? You were being what we taught you to be! Open to others. I can truthfully say, being in that situation, I doubt if I would find such success!" Frances returned her attention to the creek.

A breeze gently flirted with her hair. To Lydia, Frances Marie Wallace Burscot, was the most beautiful creature in the world. More beautiful than the girl in blue pointe shoes.

"Ok, what did I think? Hmm—let me see. Ok, you dated one man for a few years. He took you to Louisiana, to meet his family."

"That was Mitchell. Ugh. You talk about a walking nightmare! Daddy had a habit of calling him monkey face to his face yet!"

"Yes, Mitchell. Well, let's say you toughened up after that one. He was too weak for you. Too weak. Since he possessed no strength, he tried to manipulate and occasionally succeeded. Very bad news! I sincerely believe he would have physically hurt you, and I do mean badly. Despite all of that, I think

Mitchell really loved you. Perhaps that was the problem. He loved you too much."

"Maybe so. A few years after we broke up, he apologized for the hurt. I don't know. Daddy never liked him. Like I said, Daddy would called him names, and instead of standing by my man, I just laughed! I paid for that later! Mitchell had a temper!"

"Dee called 'em as he saw 'em. Your dad saw a big monkey dating his little girl!

"Ha! I finally got rid of him! It is too bad, that Mitchell thought he had to be Mister Boss Man. When he came down from that perch, he was very sweet. Unfortunately, he didn't trust enough in himself!"

"That's true, but you were better away from him, right?"

Mother does know best

"Ok, now let's see. Oh, yes, there was that engineer. If things hadn't worked for you and Seth, the engineer would've been great! Seth, though, he's the one. He is the cream of the crop!"

"That's funny—"

"Why, baby?"

Lydia reviewed the creek's ripples. "Jewel says the same thing about him. She liked him from the start. On our first date she saw Seth open the car door for me and she was hooked."

"Great minds *do* think alike. " Lydia groaned as her mother continued to sermonize. "Now, Seth's road has been bumpy too. He's worked so hard to make it this far. Your life together, will be glorious! Remember, get use to that kitchen! Bake him up a pie or two, ok? He'll be yours for more than a lifetime!"

Lydia smiled and nodded. The air chilled more. She preferred to talk indoors, but was afraid to mention it. Wonder if this dream would end? She didn't want that.

"There was one time, though, I wanted to kick a man just where it hurt! His behavior towards you, betrayed any trust you had in him!"

She's talking about Junior,. I needed her then. Where was she? "You knew about him?" Lydia unknowingly panicked.

"That poor excuse of a man! You weren't more than four-teen. He and your dad planned a night out and wanted some liquor before they left. Junior offered to get them some, while Dee finished getting ready. You wanted to ride along. That wasn't a big deal, since Junior was like a big brother to you. He always loved tickling you when you were small. For glory's sake, Junior even took you to your dance lessons! You had absolutely no reason to distrust him, did you?"

Why can't you leave this alone? You weren't there to help me. What difference does it make now? You just weren't there when I needed you!

"On the way home, from the liquor store, Junior stopped on Rawson Street, and cut the lights. Out of the blue, he held your hand. He intertwined his gigantic fingers with yours. You were fourteen years old and this grown man was holding on to you! Junior tried to kiss and touch you! My wrath was strong as much as your trust was destroyed. You stood up for yourself and told him to stop. A light flickered in his head that you were serious. It could have been so much worse! You never told your dad. You were so scared."

"Yes, I figured Dad needed friends too. Even if they were scum like Junior. He didn't come round much after that. Deep down I was thrilled, but sad for Daddy."

"And Junior pops up still today."

"This summer, he was over to the house, visiting Daddy. I walked in the house, and instantly shrunk to that fourteen year old girl. He's a big wig in real estate, here in Samm County. Just weird, ya know? Nothing ever happened like that again. With him or any other man. You instilled something in my mind, *Frances!*"

"Hey, remember, that's mother, mom, any variation there of, to you, kiddo!" Frances, laughingly warned. "I am so proud of you, for sticking to your guns!"

Lydia stretched and wrapped her arms around herself. The air nipped at her. She eased closer. She needed to be closer to her. To Mama. "Mama, what about your surgery? Why? There was no reason you had to die!"

"Lydia, when God calls your number, he calls your number. You gotta answer—not put Him on hold."

"Sure, ok, I'll buy that. But what made you decide?" the October wind iced Lydia's skin and she huddled closer.

"As I said before, Rose and Starr had success. I felt this was my last shot at it. Baby, didn't we cover this at the house?"

"Yes, we did. Still nags at me—sorry." Lydia actually was sorry for bringing this up again. None of this bode well—if it ever would. "Mama, nobody wanted you to have that surgery. You'd lost weight before. So why?" Lydia's voice rose. "I think it was a cop out, Mama. Afterward, you were so sickly. You never bounced out of it. You gagged just putting in your dentures, for godsakes! You lost a few pounds, but was the ultimate result worth it? Didn't you care what you did to us?"

"Lydia, of course, I cared about you! Don't ever doubt that! I made a choice. I wanted to survive—but it wasn't meant to be. I thought it would work!"

"Mama, what you were successful at, was making a thirteen year old a motherless child! Wow, now isn't *that* something to be proud of?" *Why am I doing this? I want it to stop! Why does she keep looking at the creek?*

"Baby, I loved our dad. I loved *you*. You were my entire world. I was so very proud of the young woman you were growing up to be. I wanted you to be proud of me!"

"Mama, I was proud of you! Oh my God, you threw it all away!" snapped Lydia. "You threw it all away, dammit! Me and daddy! You gave up your whole, entire life! And for what?" Lydia welded her body to her mother's, yet her mother kept her gaze on the creek. Silence. *Why doesn't she look at me? I thought she loved me?*

Lydia inspected her mother's profile again. Was it only a few moments ago, Frances Marie Wallace Burscot was the most beautiful person in the world? How could it all change? Why did she want to hurt her mother more than she'd ever been hurt herself?

•◆•

Without warning, Lydia let her words became sarcastic darts brushed with poison. "You didn't answer me, *Frances*. Oops, sorry! That oughta be mother, mom, or some variation there of, right? Anyway, what did you give your life up for? Huh? Huh? Let's see, oh yes, a box, six feet under? Granted, it was quite the pretty box, that Daddy had to pay an arm and a leg for! A box in the cold, dark ground? With a dried up rose and worms to keep you company? Tell me, *Frances*, was it worth it? Oh, come now—not having the chance to see your only child grow up? Not much to give up, huh? The very same child, you gave birth to after suffering through four miscarriages! You gave up hugging her, loving her, teaching her to avoid life's little pitfalls. Yep, not much, right, *Frances*? And for what, *Frances*? A big ol' wooden box! Certainly something I would strive for! What's the matter, *Frances*, cat, or should say worm, got your tongue?"

Lydia knew her voice soared above the crickets as she yanked on Frances' left arm. They must be face to face. She had to look into the eyes of the woman, who said she loved her, but decided to leave her. "What do you have to say, *Frances*? Oops, there I go again! Not a very good variation, huh? Sorry!" Lydia knew she walked with fire. "Ok, sure, we've had these cool little mother-daughter chit chats. Actually, some have been quite nice. But, *Frances*, what did you expect? I mean, let's check the calendar. You've been dead nearly thirty years! So you figured, I'd have the welcome wagon out, huh? Get real, mommy dearest!"

Lydia squeezed Frances' arm. There was no resistance. Lydia wanted Frances Marie Wallace Burscot to feel even the slightest hint of pain. Lydia glared into the eyes of the person that gave her life. "Well, *Frances*, you have anything to say? I'm sure the clock is ticking away, and you'll be doing the dust to dust thing real soon, huh?"

"Lydia, come on, now. Calm down. Let's sit down. I made a mistake—"

"Oh, lookee here, the woman speaks. And she says she made a mistake? Isn't that so nice. A mistake? You made a mistake, all right, *Frances*, by coming here tonight! Couldn't you have left well enough alone? Did you have to come and hurt me more?" Lydia's voice soared above the crickets' chirps. Her lungs pushed against her ribs. "A mistake is something you make in your checkbook! What you did, *Frances*, was selfish and cruel!" Lydia squeezed as hard as she could. She wanted to cut off circulation—*if there was any blood to cut off.*

"How dare you? Bitch! You can't even speak truth! You know you're wrong! You selfish bitch! You were proud of me—for what? You said yourself you weren't around to guide me. Assist me, with life's little pitfalls, as you put it! Then school. Ha! What about *before* school? You smacked my hands because my finger-nails weren't as luscious as yours? Look at em, now *Frances*! Look good don't they? Yep, and they only cost me twenty-five dollars! How bout that, *Frances*?" The night air became Lydia's energy source. .

"Let's go one step further, why don't we, *Frances*? How about the morning, you ripped an entire dress off me? Com-plete-ly OFF me! You hollered and screamed for me to take it all off! You were crazed and I was petrified! Did you care? Obviously not! Your perfectly manicured, polished hands seized that plaid dress from my body. There I was, standing on a chair, and miraculously, I kept my balance! Wonder if I had fallen, *Frances*? Then what? How would you explain that? What a hate-ful woman! Suddenly, I go from being fully clothed, to slip and panties. Why would a mother do that, *Frances*? Me, your only child, scared, crying and screaming, all at the same time! I thought you were determined to hurt me as much as you could!" Contempt, not blood, raced through Lydia's veins. "You went to my closet, pulled out something, threw it at me, made some snide comment about it fitting. I, then, trotted off to Webster School, as if nothing occurred. I was devastated! Somehow I made it through the day, *Mommy*. Is that a good variation for you? Gee, I was terrified to walk through our own front door that afternoon! How did I know you weren't going to really hurt me? Did you know that, *Frances*?"

"Lydia, baby, I was wrong. Come on, let's—"

"Let's what? Have a tea party? No! You shut up and listen!" Lydia clinched her teeth and kept her mother's arm in her grasp. "Ok, so Daddy wasn't the encouragement pusher, you were.

Hey, Daddy tried. At least, *he hung around*. More than you can say, huh? You pushed me to be whatever *you* desired. Nothing I dreamt of! How come you didn't know I wanted to dance? Weren't you the woman with the grand intuition? Then when I wanted to take French, *ooooh boy*! You thought that was the funniest thing! Just because *you* had no clue, didn't mean you should put down my choice. *My* choice!"

Lydia shook her mother's arm back and forth. *I have to make you listen. You haven't heard me in almost thirty years.* "MY choice! MY choice, Mama! NOT yours!" Lydia's soul was ablaze. "To get thin, you chose surgery! All you had to do, *Frances*, was cut down on sweets and greasy concoctions, and voila, *c'est fait*! Oops! *C'est francais, Mamam*. Just think, after giving up those few little passions, pounds would've poured off! You couldn't do that, now could you? Nope, our little Franny decided to take her own way. Sure, sure, the being independent thing works here, but, now, what was this surgery? Oh yea, was some of your intestine removed? One little organ we sure don't need, huh?" Lydia smoked her opinions into her mother's face. "And of course, continuing on your independent course, you possessed every complication known to the free world! What was the final chorus, *Frances*? A teensy weensy little liver problem? Let's see, I think the correct name for it was acute yellow liver atrophy. Ya know, *Frances*, there I was, thirteen, looking at your death certificate, and then grabbing the dictionary. I had to look up the words to see what killed my mother. Something that could have been avoided. But, oh now, we had to be a size sixteen or was it a fourteen, *Frances*? You gave up your only child, a man that adored you, and a full life, for an early grave. Wise choice, mother dear!"

Lydia grabbed her mother's sweatshirt and yanked her closer—till the tips of their noses touched. Lydia wanted her eyes to scorch any remnants of Frances Marie Wallace Burscot's soul.

•◆•

The night began with such joy and promise. Now anger, and disappointment circled like vultures waiting for the kill. There was no reason this should be happening. Nothing signaled a change would occur. Why was the air suddenly so cold? Lydia longed to cradle in her mother's arms, yet she wanted to strangle her equally as much.

How can I strangle an already dead person? I could try for history, or at least the cover of grocery store tabloid. "Have you nothing to say, Mama? Nothing at all?" Frances, with her gaze fixed on Lydia, remained silent. "Say something! Say SOME-THING! You bitch!"

Lydia grabbed Frances' other arm and, again, began shaking. The breeze from her mother's body wave back and forth cooled her. "You were so selfish! You didn't care about what you left behind! You *chose* to commit suicide. The only difference was, it took you three months to die, instead of an instant! "Say something! You didn't care! You just didn't care!" Lydia's eyes rimmed with hot tears. They felt like blood. "I loved you once! You were my mother. You did this to Daddy and me! You did this to ME! The sight of you makes me sick! Do you hear me? Do you hear me, *Frances*? You make me sick! YOU-MAKE-ME-SICK!"

In one swift motion, Lydia stopped the shaking, and slammed her palm against Frances' left cheek. "You BITCH!"

•◆•

Instantly, Lydia realized her actions. "Oh my God! What have I done?" Sobs choked her and to inhale, nearly broke her insides. Lydia flung both hands over her mouth. Bile inched its way to freedom as she tiptoed backward. Lydia's eyes remained on her mother. *Why doesn't she soothe her cheek? I wanted to hurt her as much as she did me, that one morning.*

Lydia took another step backward. She wanted to run. The darkness became a tilt to whirl ride at the carnival. Her right heel caught something and she tumbled to the ground. Lydia tried to gather herself together. With her elbows resting on her knees, Lydia placed her chin on a clenched fist. She silently demanded her head to quit spinning.

How could something so evil possess Lydia's complete being. Why? The rage—where had it come from? Why did she say those awful things? So hateful! Words, that spewed from her own mouth, shocked and sickened her. No denying, the voice belonged to her. Hers! Yet, the fire that ignited—

None of this could be happening! None of it! How can I slap Mama? This visit, this dream, started out to be more than I ever wanted. I'm with Mama again. Why did I do this?

• ◆ •

What time was it anyway? A wedding—HER wedding was planned for the next day. *No, this day.* She had to go home. She had to wake up—

"Lydia? Lydia? Are you all right? Did you hurt yourself?"

That voice. This nightmare was not close to being over. That fragrance closed in. The voice was above her. A hand traced through her hair.

"Lydia." The caress relaxed her. "Baby, I am so sorry. You're right, I gave up the world, for what I thought was the shot of a life time. I thought that's what it would take for me to be happy. I was so wrong. Dead wrong. It was my choice. A choice, if I could do over, I would. You and your dad were my entire world. I thought I was enhancing it. I don't expect you to understand. I'm not sure I do. I've caused you so much pain. I missed all those important events with you. A mother is suppose to be there for her baby. I let you down, because of a choice I made. I am so sorry, baby. So sorry. Now please, get up off this ground. Please let me help you."

Half of Lydia yearned to scream again, but the other side, exhausted, kept her from it. She didn't want to fight anymore. Lydia took the hand in silence, and rose to her knees. She wouldn't permit herself to look up.

Lydia felt her hand being squeezed, she fell back on her knees. "I-I can't do this. I've had enough. I want to go home!" Tears stung Lydia's eyes. On her face, Lydia felt the warmth of a palm. The palm gently stroked her and gave her strength to rise to her knees. Without thought, Lydia's arms wrapped around her mother's waist and buried her face in her mother's belly. The security of her mother's arms enclosed her. This was Lydia's life preserver. She knew that.

"Baby." Lydia heard sorrow. "Baby, I am sorry. So sorry. I hope one day you can believe that. God gifted you to me. You were my angel and I made a choice which prevented me from experiencing my gift to its fullest extent! It was my fault for not being there, to watch you soar. I am so sorry. *So sorry.*" Frances kept repeating the last two words. Lydia's grasp on her mother's waist tightened.

I must not let go. Ever.

"Get up, Lydia. Come out of the wet grass. Let's go sit on a table." Frances pulled her from the ground.

The back of Lydia's hand substituted for tissue. Would these tears ever stop?

Frances scrambled to a table's top. "C'mon sit up here. You must be cold."

That Lydia could not deny. She trembled in her damp sweats and sat beside Frances. Lydia surprised herself, that after the abuse she'd thrown, she still reached to clasp her mother's hand. She then rested her head on her mother's shoulder. She was so very tired. So sleepy now.

"I slapped you. I slapped you. And you didn't kill me. Why didn't you?" The words were difficult to form. No screams. No sarcasm. Only fatigue.

"Well, daughter, you smacked me pretty good, if I do say so myself. I deserved it. The rage has built up for a long time. There is no way I can fault you. I left you. I abandoned you at a time most precious. I deserved whatever you dish out to me—"

"Really?" Lydia's head remained on her mother's shoulder. She fought sleep.

"You are right, you know. In everything you said. Also, you got back at me for all the pain caused, whether verbal or even physical." Frances took a deep breath. "And that dress episode—I was ashamed of what I did. I was a person possessed. It goes back to me. My desire of being thin. I wanted you to share that too."

"Mama, I was ok the way I was."

"Were you really? Be serious!"

Lydia paused. "Ok, well, I hated it when we got weighed in grade school. Belle Glover was in my class. She was always bigger than me. That made me feel better. Mama, if you had dealt with it differently—"

"I didn't know how! I pushed for what I wanted. Not what *you* wanted. It was the only way I knew how." For the first time that night, Lydia heard Frances' voice rise. "I was determined to get the weight off you. I felt the pounds would hinder you as time wore on."

"My God, mother! My weight only hindered me when I let it! You preached about independence. Was that a lesson meant to be used around everyone else, in every other situation, except you?" Lydia straightened. She hoped the urge to sleep would disappear and squeezed her mother's hand, to make it so.

"Maybe so. I wanted everything for you. Things I didn't have. I wanted you to see things my way."

"Mother, I did see things your way—and *my* way. You and Daddy taught me to be my own person. That meant even around you. There couldn't be a double standard."

"I guess one must be careful what they ask for, right?" Frances pulled Lydia closer.

Lydia relaxed in her mother's grasp. This was the sort of memory she wanted to tuck away for safe keeping. "I'd like to change the subject, Mama, if you don't mind."

"Honey, that's fine. Anything you want."

"Ok, I have to ask you somethin'—"

"Ha! There's a 'g' at the end of that word, girl!"

"Huh? Oh, Mama, really! I'm not twelve anymore!"

"Yes, I know, dear. I know."

Is that remorse I hear? "Do you recall the day I asked you about liking a white boy, those many years ago?"

"Ha! Ha! Yes, I sure do! Seth was the boy you asked about, wasn't he?"

Lydia nodded and smiled. "Yes, he's the one."

"When you asked me, I was caught so off guard!"

"What? You were? I don't believe it! You were so cool to my friends! How could you be caught off guard?"

"Oh, I knew it was coming around the bend. I was surprised it hit our front door so fast! I must have made about twenty tons of noodles that day!"

Lydia found energy to laugh and heard Frances do the same. This is how Lydia wanted it. No anger, nor sadness. Just the two of them, together.

"Oh, the look on your face that day! You were ready to bust!" Frances laughed harder. "I knew we were officially into the hormone game. This was serious stuff. Remember, I left to go get your dad from work? He and I discussed it on the way home"

"You guys talked about it? I never knew!" For some reason, Lydia was embarrassed. "What did Daddy have to say?"

"Oh, you know your dad. He chewed on that cigar, and relented his baby was growing up. I truly feel it was harder for him. Until that moment, he was the only man you loved. Now someone attempted to take that title away from him. Even now, your dad is wrapped around all ten of your fingers!"

"Well, I wouldn't say all of that!"

"Sure, whatever you say," Frances said, sarcastically. "Back to Seth, perhaps you knew back on that afternoon, he was going to be special to you. And wait—what was that you told me? His full name, his complete full name was Seth Jacob Delaney. With his birthday being, hmm—let me think!" Frances playfully tapped her forehead, as if to regain a vision. "Oh yes, his birthday is January 18!"

"Mama! How in the world do you remember that?" Lydia's cheeks burned.

"Ha! Ha! Oh baby! You were so precious that day! Cherish Seth with all your heart and soul! It's great how you two found each other after all this time. And that gown! Seth will be mesmerized by your beauty."

Lydia laid her head back on Frances' shoulder. Fatigue set in again. "Mama, what do you think of my choices? Are you disappointed?"

After a pause, Frances replied, "We've covered some of this already. I'm proud of you for now using the gray matter God gave you. Sure there are things, I wished you would have done by now. But the thing is, you are happy and you're great at what you do. You've tasted success. And you like it! So, I'm confident your spoon, fork, and plate will be piled high with more! You're striving to make your dreams come true. Decisions are your own. Fears have been, and always will be, conquered. The power of that gray matter will never fail you. I want happiness to always be your companion. Serious trouble is not part of your game plan. And most of all, you are so beautiful!"

"It's in the genes!" Lydia chirped.

"And you never forget that!" Frances drew her arm around Lydia. "You're sleepy aren't you?"

•◆•

"Yes. It must be late. I don't have my watch. Brrrr. The wind has picked up. The dog might be awake too!" Lydia curled closer. Their hands clasped together. The words she screamed echoed through her brain. Why had she been so selfish and stupid? She knew Mama loved her and always would.

What happened had been a choice, a bad one, but it had been a choice. Mama's choice. "The things I said to you. I-I can't believe I said those words to you. They were hateful. I mean, I cussed at you—again!" Lydia hushed. She stood two inches tall. "I am so sorry. So sorry. I've been so mad over the years. And so sad."

"I know you have, angel," Frances said, her lips brushing against Lydia's forehead. "You had to release all that anger. No matter how much it hurt the both of us. You felt abandoned. You've been by yourself for such a long time!"

Lydia's head shot up. A defensive tone caught her voice, "I have not been by myself! I had Daddy, and everybody else! You know that! I told you that!"

"Baby, calm down. Down deep, you know what I meant. You missed the guidance of a mother. There were so many things I wanted to teach you."

"But you did. You tried." Lydia unwrapped her hands from her mother's and rubbed them together. Her body shivered and fatigue caused her eyelids to droop. "You taught me how to shop. How to pick out things. I found it so boring then. Now I would savor a shopping trip with you." A yawn escaped. "And I have to know something else." *Before Mr. Sandman shovels sleep in my eyes.* "Mama—mother," Lydia attempted to stay lucid, "you taught me about female intuition. Never to fight it. Um, did your intuition tell you—" Lydia sucked in her breath. "Did it tell you—"

"Did it tell me I was going to die before you were grown? Yes, it did. I knew I wouldn't see you grown. I prayed to be wrong."

"The thought must have haunted you."

"Oh, baby, it did. I just wanted to see you grown. I wanted to fly to Arizona, to see Mae and the kids. I wanted to do alot of things."

"I remember you talking to her on the phone. Telling her how much you wanted to fly. It was right before—"

"Yes, a week or so, before I went to Lutheran Hospital that final time. And the night I was wheeled out of the house, my God—the look on your face—my baby was in so much pain. And I was helpless. Oh, I wanted to take it all back. *All of it.* I prayed you would grow into a strong, confident, and independent woman."

"But Mother, I am those things!"

"Yes, in many ways you are. I caused damage in others, that I cannot undo. All I can do, is ask for your forgiveness. Your personality traits are your focal points. They can also be your undoing. But then again, you've been able to handle what's been thrown your way. I have no need to fret."

"And that's because of you!" Lydia was content, for she knew she spoke the truth. Because of Mother, she was strong.

• ◆ •

"Maybe, we need to get back. The wind has picked up." Lydia said. "I'm getting colder by the second. And look, isn't that lightening over in the north. Great, more rain!"

"I'd like to make one more stop, if you don't mind."

"But, Mother, the wind." Lydia' s teeth chattered. "It's cold!"

"Please, baby, just one more. Humor an old woman!"

"You're not old! You're just a few years older than me! Really! Can't we go somewhere warm? And we can talk more there. I'm starting to get sleepy again." Lydia slid off the picnic table and faced Frances. "We can go home and sit upstairs. It would be just us. How about that?"

"Lydia, I don't think so. I have another place in mind."

"Ok, where?"

"Back to Violet Hill."

"What? Back to the cemetery? What on earth for? "Why there? I've been out there quite a bit lately! Thank you!"

"I know, baby. I've been out there quite a bit too!"

Why don't I think before I speak sometimes? Lydia lowered her head and walked in silence. Her arms crossed her chest. "Ok-ok-we'll have it your way. I just don't get it. You have been out there for a long time, I knew that. It just slipped out."

"I know. It's difficult since you can't fully comprehend. It's just a place I feel safe in."

"Mother, it's the middle of the night. And we're alone here in the park. I think we're on the safe side here!"

Frances chuckled. "Maybe so, but just grant your ol' Mama her wish."

As they neared Lydia's car, Frances retrieved the car keys from the pocket of her sweats. "Get in. This won't take long." Frances ignited the Mitsubishi and again, without hesitation, began to exit from Davis Park.

Within minutes they were back on Willis Avenue. A few blocks later, at the first of three stop lights in Brenner, Frances turned left. She steered north, on Second Street, with her left hand and pressed radio buttons with her right. Once they tapped onto jazz, her fingers left the radio alone.

"Nice style." Frances announced.

"Yes, it is. Very smooth."

"Better than those Osmond Brothers! What was the deal with them? Their hair was so shaggy! And all those *teeth*!"

Lydia laughed. "Oh, Mother, they were fun! And besides, the Jackson Five came through Iowa just once!"

"Sure, dear, whatever you say. You still have posters of them and their teeth hanging on a wall in that attic! Did you go and see the Jackson 5 when they came through Iowa that one, as you say, time?"

"No Mother, I didn't."

"And why not? You liked their music. Well, after I bought it for you, and made you listen to it!"

"Ha! Ha! You're right. Mama, they were at the Iowa State Fair in August of 1971. That was a month before—"

"Before I died. You had the chance and you stayed home?"

Lydia regained her voice. "Yes, I did. You were having problems. A few days before their performance, you and I had gone to Merle Hay Shopping Center for school clothes. You drove to Des Moines without your dentures. Once we got there, you tried to put them in and gagged. You vomited some too. I was scared. I wasn't sure we were going to make it home."

Frances kept her gaze on Second Street. "I just wanted to buy you some new clothes."

"That's exactly what you said that day, too." Lydia's chest stiffened.

"Oh, baby, you had to grow up so fast. You shouldn't have felt you had to stay home with me. You needed to enjoy yourself."

"Look, Mother, it happened. I have no regrets. I wanted to be with you!" Lydia reached to squeeze Frances' leg.

"You were so young—can you ever forgive me?" Frances glanced at Lydia, then returned her eyes to Second Street.

"Only if you can forgive me, Mother!" Before Lydia could give Frances time to respond, she charged onward, "Look, tell me, what do you think of the sights of Second Street?"

"Another tactic, eh? Fine." Frances glanced at Lydia and smiled. Her eyes returned to the street. "It looks like alot of stores have closed. That's sad. On Saturdays this street bustled. There was a time, people scurried to Spurgeon's or stopped for candy at Ben Franklin's 5 and 10. Then got popcorn, from that old lady, on the corner. Remember? We'd go into Rexall's Drug Store and sit at the counter for a burger. In your case, though, buy all those new teen magazines!"

"Ugh, ok, Mother. You can cut it now. Oh, but before I forget, those teen magazines? The very same teen magazines you made me burn one summer night? They are worth good money now. I've seen them at collectible shows. So there!" Lydia huffed.

Frances ignored Lydia and continued, "We took you to the library steps to meet Santa Claus. You were always scared and that was before you slit those packages open!

"Mother, really!"

"None of those stores are anywhere to be seen. I can tell that even in the dark! That's sad. Brenner should have been further ahead after all these years. Oh well, maybe one day. I came back—so certainly this street can too!"

"Now, that is the truth! Things did move out over time. Tastes changed, I suppose." Lydia was melancholy. She recalled how fun it use to be running amuck on Second Street. It seemed so full of life, just like her mother, once upon a time.

"Baby, are you all right? You got quiet all of sudden." Frances sounded concerned.

"I was remembering those times too. Just seems so long ago." Lydia sighed. "Mother, with Daddy working at the pork plant, and me in school all day, why didn't you go on to nursing school? You were smart and good with people."

Silence. She watched her mother pull in her bottom lip and then release it. "I don't know Lydia. Perhaps the times. Or I was scared of failing. Maybe I thought I was too old."

"Mother, how can you say that? You were my age then! You weren't old by any means!" *How can Mama be afraid of anything? Tilda always said she was the coolest Mama around!*

"Back then a grown woman wasn't given much encouragement to switch gears. But, by your reaction I can see that has changed too!"

"I thought you watched over me? How could you not know about those kinds of changes?"

"Honey, calm down. Yes, I watched over you, not the *world*."

"Yea, ok, I get that. Oh, Mother, you should have gone. You would have been so good, and so much happier! What did Daddy say?" Lydia hated to admit times were different. *That's why she stressed so hard for me to be independent and follow my dreams.*

"Oh, your daddy—you know him! He told me to do whatever it took to be happy. He didn't hold me back. Dee is wonderful in that regard. He had less than I did growing up. I'm the one that held back!"

"You're so honest about it. Being scared and all. I don't know what to say."

"Lydia, why should I lie to you? You're a grown woman. There is no reason to keep secrets. Perhaps, if we had grown up together, God only knows what I'd be right now!"

•◆•

The Diamante made its way into the cemetery's entrance. Lydia wasn't surprised as they parked beside her mother's headstone. Frances turned off the ignition, but made no motion to exit..

"Any regrets, Mother? About not going to nursing school, I mean?"

Frances leaned back on the headrest and caressed the steering wheel. Then she turned her head to Lydia. "Any regrets, baby? Yes, of course. I could have been so much more. I could have made myself proud. That was what I lacked. The pride in myself!"

"Oh, come on! Lydia was dumbfounded "You were the proudest woman I knew!" "Mother, how in the world can that be true?"

"Perhaps if I had followed my own dreams, instead of pushing them onto you—I would have avoided the surgery, and not have conjured up my biggest regret—not watching you grow up. Also perhaps, my feeling of *not* surviving would have washed away. That's something only God knows."

Tears trickled down Frances' cheek. Lydia pushed them away with a finger. "Come on, baby, let's get out." Frances opened the door and stepped out.

Lydia followed in silence. The lump in her throat prevented her from speaking.

"This is the most peaceful place in town. Safe." Frances stood in the open space between the car and her own headstone. Her arms stretched above her head, while her neck arched back. She drank in the rain cleansed air, as if tasting it for the first time.

"Driving felt so good! Thanks for trusting me with your Mitsu-*whatever* it was. Ahh, and think if there was time. The places we would go! Just the two of us! You and me! Just drive. Like we use to do, when your daddy fished. Our freedom of being just two girls on the prowl. Tasty Treat ice cream, hot dogs, and maybe your latest addiction, onion rings from the A & W, in tow!"

Lydia laughed at the long ago memory of their roadtrips. "Yep, those were the days! Fun, too! So what now, Mother? I've been hearing thunder."

"So are you scared? Being out here, in the cemetery, so late? This place spooked you once upon a time."

Lydia swore her mother's eyes twinkled. "Geesh, I was six years old and my great big cousins, Ronnie and Butch threatened to leave me out here! I'm beyond that now!"

"You sure? And I also seem to recall you being deathly afraid of their outhouse. You'd wet the bed just so you wouldn't—"

"*Mother!*" Lydia's rolled her eyes in exasperation.

"Ok, ok, I hear you. You tired?"

"Actually, I am. It's been a long night. I know I have to get up sometime soon. What time is it anyway?"

"We'll only be here a minute or two. Come over this way, baby." Lydia followed Frances to a row of three smaller headstones. "These people loved you so much. And they miss you too. You are never far from their hearts. Never forget that."

Lydia knew they stood by the graves of her aunts, Mary and Grace, and Uncle Hippy. They were her family. How could she forget them? They'd taken her under wing when Mama died. Always there.

Hippy always made her laugh. When he tried to pull one over on her, his dimples gave him away. Lydia could not be a full fledged Burscot, he claimed, until she handled a shot of whiskey. Of course, that first shot scorched her throat, along with every organ in her body. Hippy informed her they would keep her—for now anyway.

In later years, their relationship deepened. He loved telling her about the Burscot side of the family. And, oh how Lydia loved to listen! When sister Grace died, he gave up. They both lived in the house they were born in, and Grace died there. Marriage did not find either one of them. They were as devoted as any brother and sister.

Mary, the eldest, made the best macaroni and melted butter in the world. When Mama died Mary took to the task of using the hot comb on Lydia's wash and dried hair. One Sunday, Lydia called Mary to ask if she had time to press it. Mary was in the middle of something and wasn't able to. Lydia thought Mary sounded irritated, and never asked her again. Lydia didn't want to be a bother to anybody.

When Mary asked why she wasn't coming by anymore, to get her hair done, Lydia announced she was able to do it all by herself. Thirteen year old Lydia was determined to prove how grown up she was. She didn't need anybody.

Now, the nearly forty year old, Lydia hid sobs by sucking in her bottom lip. Her head pounded like a core of drums. They just kept getting louder, just like the thunder in the distance.

"My angel, I need to get you home."

"No, I want to stay! I want to stay with you! I want more time!" Lydia wiped away tears with her sleeve. Her guise was that of a thirteen year old's. "Are you going to stay with me? Through the night? You can't go, Mama! Not again!"

"Lydia, come on. You have to go home! There's a wedding that's going to be happening, and you are the star!" Frances attempted to guide Lydia to the car.

"Mother, I hate for this to end! Don't let it! This has been too short. There's many more things I want to talk about! It's been thirty years!" Lydia was breathless and her body ached from exhaustion. This dream must keep moving! This was her mother. Her Mama. It couldn't end.

"Lydia, come on baby. There may be another time."

"Another time? Really? Oh, Mother, do you promise?"

"Lydia," Frances guided Lydia back to her own headstone. "I am always here for you," she whispered. "Touch this stone, touch my soul. Say your words. I hear your love. Never, never doubt that!"

"But-but-Mama! Please! Not again. It's just so hard!" Not again!" Lydia flung herself into her mother's chest. Her own chest heaved with sobs.

Frances cradled Lydia's head and held her close. "Baby, you've lived and you will continue to live. You're a strong woman. Always remember that. There are people, who love you, that protect you, and God forever watches you. You, Lydia, are well taken care of. Just do use that gray matter you were gifted with, then there will be no failure. Believe that."

Lydia wanted to believe. Maybe one day she would, only now, this moment in time, is what she worried about. Lydia was

determined to hang on. With eyes shut tightly, the scent of Straw
Hat swirled within her nostrils. She would never let go. Mama
wouldn't leave her again. Not this time.

Rain splashed on Lydia's cheek. She didn't care. Her tummy
twisted into knots, which made her grasp tightened.

"Lydia? Honey, look at me."

Lydia shook her head.

"Come on. Baby, it's ok. Look at me." Frances gently pushed
Lydia away. "*Thomasina!*"

Lydia shot her head up. Her eyes flooded with water. Was
the water, her tears or rain? She stared into her mother's own tear
stained eyes. Rain splattered harder upon them. Lydia reached to
caress her mother's face. She wanted to capture a memory with
her fingertips. The softness of her mother's skin. These thoughts,
these memories, would warm her during cold times.

Lydia's index finger wiped tears and rain from Frances'
cheek. This moment had to be savored. Contentment inched its
way through Lydia, as she felt her mother's hands cup her face.
Thunder crashed as lightening bolts flickered to the north.

"You are my heart, Lydia AnMarie Burscot. Never forget that!
You were and are my life. You are a strong, independent woman.
I could be no more proud. You can and you will go on."

Lydia's lips quivered. She heard the heaviness in her
mother's voice. Lydia wrapped her fingers around the Frances'
arms, and leaned forward enough for their heads to touch. The
battle was fruitless. No possible way to win. Frances wrapped
Lydia in her arms and Lydia nuzzled under the secure spot of her
mother's chin. Rain fused them together. *We will always be
together, you and I.*

Frances cleared her throat. "Baby, at night, just before you
fell asleep, do you remember what I would say to you?"

"Y-yes. It's been a long time," the lump in Lydia's throat held
her words in check. "I thought I'd never hear you say it again."
There were words she had to say—words she didn't say the first
go-round. When she was thirteen. Before everything changed.
Lydia pulled herself back and looked into her mother's eyes and
whispered, "I love you, Mama. Please, believe me. I love you!"

Lydia watched tears stream from the corners of her mother's eyes. There it was again—heat rose up her spine. It comforted her. She knew all would be fine. Lydia felt her mother's lips press against her forehead. These arms were safe, secure, warm. Lydia was at peace. The heat in her spine spread throughout her body. She hugged harder, and rested under her mother's chin.

"Always remember, Lydia, *Mama love.*"

"I know. I know."

A smile crept across Lydia's face. This is where she wanted to be. A clap of thunder rocked the Earth. Its impact went by, ignored by mother and daughter.

•◆•

"Lydia! Lyd-DEE-a! Get your butt out that bed, girl! We got us a wedding to get ready for today!"

What? Who was that yelling? Wedding? Huh? Someone gently shook her. Daddy.

"Girl, get out that bed. You've slept too late as it is. C'mon. I'm gonna make you some of my special weddin' day pancakes!"

Daddy? What? The room spun as she tried to sit up. Bed? What was she doing in bed? Wasn't she at Violet Hill Cemetery moments ago? It started to rain, hadn't it? Wasn't she hugging Mama, when a giant clap of thunder shook the ground? Lydia rubbed her temples.

"Sweety, you ok?"

"Oh yea, Daddy just trying to wake up. Just nerves."

Lydia looked down and saw her body covered with her flannel nightshirt. The same one she put on last night. What happened to her sweat suit?

"Well, you and the devil dog must have had a night!"

"What makes you say that?" Lydia asked as she reached for her glasses. The world surely would be in focus then.

"Well, I got up during the night to use the bathroom, and as usual your light was still on." Dee pretended annoyance and rolled his eyes. "So I came in here, and you and Jangles were both snoring your butts off! He was stretched out right beside you!" He found humor in his discovery. "And I even had to take off that cute little Hawkeye sweater he had on! You got that for him didn't you? Sure was cute!"

Color drained from Lydia's face. *Sweater? I didn't get any such sweater!* "Uh, you turned off the light? And we were snoring?" How could this be? She hadn't slept at all this night, had she? Lydia reached for her robe. "About what time was that, Daddy? Turning out the light, I mean?" Even with her glasses on, things still were fuzzy. "And where's Jangles now?"

"Oh, the devil dog is outside. Just let him out a little bit ago. Sure you're ok? You still seem kinda wobbly."

"Oh, Daddy, always taking care of me. I have a good case of butterflies, that's all! Now, what time did you say you turned out the light?" Lydia wrapped her robe around her as she walked into the living room. She glanced at the attic stairs.

"Oh, it was about half past midnight or so."

What? Half past midnight? Lydia's eyes widened. She was faint. Wasn't it twelve-thirty when she and Mama were headed toward the Tasty Treat? Now Daddy said it was the twelve-thirty when he shut off the light! That settled it. Everything had been a dream. All a bittersweet dream. Lydia stumbled against the arm of the recliner. "Oh, I must really have the shakes about all this wedding stuff, huh?"

Still with watchful eye, Dee lit up a cigar. "Sweety, it's going on eight now, we've still got time before we all have to get ready. So you'll have all those butterflies rid off. Now time for weddin' day pancakes!"

"Dee, all that sugar in that syrup! You know better than that!" rang Jewel.

"Woman, we have that sugarless syrup, so I'm fine!" barked Dee.

He will always be the monarch of his palace—and mine.

"And mornin' to you baby! Jewel hugged and kissed her. "You ready for the big day?" Jewel asked as she opened the refrigerator door.

"Yea, I think so."

"Uh-oh!" Lydia and Dee turned toward Jewel.

"What's the matter?" asked Lydia.

"Well, if you want milk, and I know you do, baby, we're out. And not a whole lot of butter either. In all the scurry with the wedding, I guess I forgot a few things yesterday."

"You'd forget your head, sometimes, woman!" yelped Dee.

Jewel and Lydia both rolled their eyes. "I'll run to Fareway and get some." Jewel said.

"Naw, that's ok. Let me throw on something and go. I want a newspaper anyway. The morning looks so pretty and I want to get out in it, one last time as a single woman. Since there's time, I'll ride my bike.

"You and that bike! I just can't believe you brought it all the way from Texas!" Dee said.

Lydia just laughed. How would he have excepted her in-line skates? Maybe next spring, when she'd bring him apples from Seventh Street, she'd introduce them to him. "It'll feel good. Won't take me long. Let me just go and put something on." Lydia threw on the first thing her hands touched.

"Oh, baby! You sure you want to wear those sweats?" Jewel asked.

"Huh? What's the matter with them?" Lydia was puzzled by Jewel's tone.

Dee appeared out of the kitchen. His cigar slid to the other side of his mouth. "Girl, what in the world did you fall in?"

"What are you guys talking about?" She tried to hold on to Jangles, as he barked and jumped on the door. *He did this last night and no one heard him, why didn't you hear him then?*

"You must've fallen down. Your whole butt is dried mud. There's some on your right leg too." Dee replied.

"You better go change into another pair, baby." Jewel suggested.

"Oh, yea, I forgot. I'll go change." Lydia hoped they didn't see her shake. Lydia put on another pair of sweats and headed out the door. Hey eyes widened at the sight of her car.

The lower half, of the white Diamante, had traces of dried mud. Where did it come from? Violet Hill Cemetery had gravel paths, but Lydia's car was in the same exact spot she parked it last night and she didn't think there was that much splattering when she and Jangles left it. Oh, well, she'd clean it later. The morning was too beautiful to worry about such things.

Lydia began peddling down Third Street. The dream had been something. Yes, slapping her mother, but she had been forgiven. Evidently she woke up around midnight, and Daddy turned out the light later. Yes, that was it.

The October sun beat down on her face. It felt wonderful. Hardly a car had passed her. This was the beauty of living in a small town. She and Seth may have to rethink their plan of living in Texas for another year. Or just find a much smaller place than Dallas, but it would never be Brenner. The ride to Fareway was ten blocks. The ride seemed to refresh her.

She locked her bike to one of Fareway's posts, and dashed through the store. Hardly took any time at all. While she situated the groceries in her backpack someone tapped her on the shoulder.

"Lyd?" Shouldn't you be home, being all nervous, and getting ready for this ceremony of yours?" It was an old high school mate, Dana. He stood with his wife Kee.

Dana would always be remembered as the doll who tapped her eighteenth birthday party kegs . He also began the collection for the bouquet of three and a half dozen red roses, her classmates presented her with that night. His equally beautiful spouse, Kee, was just as special. She gave birth to their second son, on Lydia's birthday, a dozen years ago. All three former classmates hugged and smiled broadly.

"Say, Lyd, were you out on Willis last night?" Dana asked.

"Huh? What makes you ask?" Lydia tried to mask her surprise.

"Well, let's see—what time were we coming back from Des Moines, honey?" Dana asked Kee. "It was about midnight or so, wasn't it?"

"More like half past, Dana. I looked at my watch wondering who in the world would also be out on the streets that time of night!"

Lydia shivered. "W-w-what made you think it was me? It was pretty dark and all."

"Because I saw those outta state plates. I thought they said 'Texas.' It was a big ol' car like what I've seen you drive. So I figured it had to be you."

Lydia gulped hard. How in the world could Dana have seen her? Daddy said he turned off her lights at twelve thirty. But the sweater that Jangles had on. This was supposed to be a dream. Then Lydia remembered the set of headlights that passed them—

"And it looked like there were two of you in the car! You weren't tripping out on Seth were ya? For one last fling?" Dana laughed.

"Oh, no, you silly!" Lydia regained her composure. Just tell them the truth. *Sort of.* "Yea, I was out and about. An old girl-friend and I were headed out to the Tasty Treat!" She faked a giggle.

"Yea, uh-huh, to see TZ. You had a big crush on him!"

"Dana! Just leave Lyd alone." Kee tugged Dana's arm. "Lyd, just ignore him. He's just mad because he didn't hold out for you!"

The former schoolmates laughed.

Kee continued, "We need to get on home. Tosha is home from college, and heaven forbid, the boys would help her, and themselves, to get their own breakfast! You have a big day ahead, Lyd! You'll be a beautiful bride! We can't wait to see you come down that aisle!"

"Yea, no kiddin' I'll have to drown my sorrows in my beer!" Dana stated sarcastically. "Ya know, we haven't had this big of a party since, oh, I don't know, since that eighteenth birthday of yours! That was a hell of a party!"

"He's right Lyd. You're the only person, in town, that could have a party in the *middle* of town, cops going past, and not get busted!"

Lydia continued to laugh. "Yea, Dad was so scared he was going to be hauled off to jail. Everyone was under age!"

"Your daddy, oh Lyd! We found out how much he loved you that night. He told everybody that if you had moved to wherever your family was, he would have died of loneliness." Kee said.

Lydia lowered her head for a second. Her smile widened. She lifted it to her friends. "Dad told the truth. I know I'm blessed. As for the party tonight, he won't have to worry. Nobody will be underage!"

"Yea, we know, dammit!" sighed Dana. "We better get going. See you at the church, Lyd! Don't be late or we'll start the party without you!"

This was just the thing Lydia needed. She hugged her old chums good-bye and watched them walk towards their car. She crouched down,. to give attention to unlocking her bike from the post. Someone brushed up against and she wound up on her bottom. "Hey!"

"Uh, we sorry, missy." a male voice said.

Lydia looked up, but the sun made her squint. She could not make out the person who apologized. It looked like a black, elderly couple stood to the side of her. She couldn't make out their faces. 'Oh, it's ok. I was in your way. I'm sorry."

"You all right?" the man asked.

"Yes, I'm fine." Lydia pulled herself up and finished unlocking her bike. The couple remained. "Uh, anything wrong?"

"No, missy, just makin' sho you ok."

"I assure you, I'm fine. Now, if you will excuse me, I need to get on home, before this butter melts." Lydia readied herself to peddle. The sun still prevented her from making out their faces. "Have a good day. Uh, bye."

"G'bye, missy." the man said.

Lydia peddled through the parking lot. What a strange little couple. She turned her head, and they were nowhere in sight. Well, they're a strange, *fast,* little couple.

The breakfast of pancakes and lively chatter was great. Jewel presented her with the last batch of fresh strawberries. Great indeed! Shortly, thereafter, the festivities began. Continuous phone calls and visits from family and friends. Well wishers all.

Somewhere along the way, Seth zipped by. "Ya ready?" he taunted.

They stood, face to face, in her parents' drive way. "Oh, I guess so. Only the Sultan of Brunei phoned. He asked if I could jet over and help him spend some of his money!"

"Oh, he did, did he? And what did you tell the good majesty?" Seth raised an eyebrow.

"That I was scheduled to marry some guy today."

"Oh, some guy, huh?"

"Yea, I told the ol' Sultan that this guy was kinda cute and even taught me how to ice skate once upon a time. So I told him, the only way I could help him spend his dough, was in the event that this guy and I ever broke up!" Lydia loved badgering Seth. He was such a good sport. "Honestly, honey, I am a trifle scared." Lydia beamed a smile that he reciprocated. "Seth, did anything crazy happen to you last night?"

"Hmm-no, I talked to my folks. Or should I say, I listened to my mother ask me, every five minutes, if I really knew what I was doing! Sheesh! Then I listened to you badger me about this zillion dollar wedding dress, that I, by the way, better absolutely adore. Or it's to divorce court for you, babe, and I'll call the Sultan, for you! Collect!"

Lydia laughed heartily.

"Then I finished phoning in my instructions to Michael Jordan, during the Bulls' game, drank some milk, and slept like a rock! Why?"

"Typical man!" Lydia softly punched his chest. "Well, I had a bizarre dream."

"Yea, like what?" He intertwined his fingers with hers.

"Well, it was about my mom."

"Your mom? Honey, she's been gone for a very long time."

"I know. I know. It was just weird. I dreamt I spent time with her last night. That we went for a drive. Walked through the park, ate ice cream."

"Huh? What? Sweetheart, that was a dream. You want your mom to be here with you today. That's only natural."

"That's true. But then Dana—"

"Lydia! It's time to get ready! Hi Seth! How ya doin' baby?" Jewel stood in the opened front door. "Come on, honey! Lacy's on her way over to do your hair. Seth, baby, we'll see you at the church, all right?" With that, the door slammed shut.

"Looks like General Jewel has sounded the alarm! I better let you go so you can get beautiful!"

"But Seth, my dream—"

"You'll have to tell me later, honey. Ok? I want to hear it. Sounds interesting." He pecked her lips, and hopped in his truck. Lydia blew him kisses as he drove off.

•◆•

The hair episode, with Lacy, went off without a hitch. Activity buzzed throughout the house and everything, amazingly, stayed on schedule. Lydia, already filled with exhaustion, realized the ceremony was still hours away. Finally, when the house quieted down, Lydia and Dee caught the last of an Iowa football game, while Jewel snored on the love seat.

"Well, girl, we're almost there!"

"Yep we are! And I'm already beat! It's been a long day, but it's just now getting started! Do you think I have time for a nap?"

"For how long?"

"It's three now, give me an hour or so. Just as long as I'm down to the church by five-thirty."

"Ok, baby, I'll wake you. No snoring though. Can't have the neighbors complain' about you today, of all days!"

Lydia smiled and stretched on the couch. If her hair flattened, Lacy would work miracles with a curling iron. Lydia desired rest. The day and that dream wore her out, yet Dana said he saw her.

•◆•

Sure enough, Daddy woke her by a gentle shake. "It's time, sweetie." Lydia placed her hand over his and squeezed.

Lydia reached for her glasses. The red, giant digital numbers read 4:15. The final countdown began. To Lydia's pleasant surprise, Jewel had a bubble bath ready for her. Her body relaxed in the peaches 'n cream scent. Just the ticket. She laid her head back on the rim, shut her eyes, smiled, and soaked. This was working out almost too well.

Her solitude was interrupted by a ringing phone. Lydia heard Jewel tell the caller she was in the tub, then silence, and then Jewel said good bye.

A knock soon followed on the bathroom door. "Baby?"

"Yes, Jewel?"

"That was TZ on the phone. He says to make sure you get his cooler back to him before you leave for your honeymoon, and any ice cream that's left. I told him, the ice cream was already in the freezer!" Jewel laughed. "I'm sure he kidded about the ice cream, but he does want his cooler back!"

Lydia's eyes flew open. The water turned to ice. His what? Ice cream in the freezer? What? Lydia nearly slid her head under water. But Lacy would pulverize her for ruining her do.

The cooler? How in the world could she have his cooler? She never saw him last night. Or had she? Dana said he saw her. But she was in bed sleeping. Wasn't she? No time to think about that. Just joking he was. Yes, that was it. Just joking. She had a wedding to get ready for. Jewel said the ice cream was in the freezer. She meant the vanilla ice cream she brought back before. Yea, that was it.

Lydia dried herself off. The peaches 'n cream fragrance cleared her senses. She threw on some loose clothes and eyed the clock. The church was seven blocks away from the house. Time certainly on her side! Lydia chuckled as she heard her parents' fussing actually rose above *Rawhide.*

Her eyes then wandered to the attic's stairs. The wedding dress awaited her and she had to get it. Daddy and Jewel were too engrossed in their own battle, and Jangles certainly was no help. She must get it. *Last night was only a dream. I just need to get the dress and be on my merry way. No problem. Just do it.*

Upstairs, everything appeared as it did last night, including her gown, which was safely behind plastic! When she *dreamt* that her mother inspected the gown, the plastic was no where in sight! Lydia shook cobwebs from her head and carefully gathered the gown. Time to get the show on the road. "Hey, guys, I'm going! See you at the church! Ok?"

The fussing stopped. "Ok, sweety! See you in a bit." Dee poked his head from the bedroom. "Love you."

The lump in Lydia's throat was now a pineapple. Butterflies flapped the reality of the situation into her. She was getting married. Tying the knot. Jumping the broom. It was finally here! Could she possibly be any more nervous?

Jangles sat at her feet, gazing up at her, and wagging his stub of a tail. "Well, puppy, this is it. The next time we walk the boulevard, I'll be a married woman!" She patted his head, and he then licked her hand and galloped back to her parents' bedroom.

Out of the front door, down the three steps, she headed for the trunk of her Diamante. As she turned the key in the trunk's lock, the thought of TZ phone call entered her mind. How could she possibly have his cooler? Last night was a *dream* afterall. There was no cooler in sight.

The trunk clicked open. As Lydia lifted the trunk, her mouth crashed to the pavement. Before her sat TZ's red, white, and blue Tasty Treat styrofoam cooler! How in the world did that get there? A joke for sure! She'd tease TZ later about it. Right now, getting to the church on time was of the essence. She was sure it was all just a gag. Nonetheless, she placed her belongings in the car, and returned to the house. Jangles, watching from the window, wagged his tail faster as Lydia stepped inside.

"Baby? Why are you back?" Dee asked. He sat at the kitchen table, sipping coffee. "You forget something?"

"I, uh, want to take a can of pop with me." Lydia hated lying. She had to check something out for herself.

"Oh, ok, Get some ice and put some in the thermos mug with the lid. Stay cold longer.

"Sure, Daddy." Lydia pulled a can of A & W Root Beer from the refrigerator door. Why was her hand trembling? She was just going to open the freezer's door.

Seven chocolate covered vanilla bars, with peanuts, stared back at her. She froze in place.

"Hee, hee, don't tell Jewel, I ate one of those bars. She'd have a hissy fit!" Dee whispered. "Ya want me to get you some ice? Don't want you to mess up those pretty fingernails you paid for!"

"Uh, no, Daddy," Lydia said as she shut the freezer door, "I'll just take the can!" Lydia hugged and kissed him, then bobbed and weaved toward the door.

"Baby, you sure you're ok?"

"Oh, Daddy, I'm fine. More than you know!" Lydia felt heat ease up her back as she made way to her car. A smile was on her face.

Lydia looked at Ms. Timex, she was due at the church in a half hour, and it was only a few blocks away. There had to be one more stop before she made her way down the aisle. This stop would only take a few minutes. She had to do it. Afterall, she was the bride—and what were they going to do? Have Reverend Terry start the proceedings without her?

Within five minutes, the Diamante steered into the gates of Violet Hill Cemetery. That was the beauty of being in a small town. Everything was five minutes away from everything. Lydia smiled at the ease of it all.

The car seemed to be on automatic pilot as it parked beside her mother's headstone. *I just can't stay away from this place.* She exited from the car and surprised herself that there was no tentativeness in her step. She knew where she had to go.

The headstone must be touched. Lydia needed to be close to *her*— whether it was a dream or not. She needed to *feel* close.

The late October sun fought its way over the horizon. It would not go quietly. Lydia thought the sun tried to shine brighter, for rays of the sun seemed to shine a spotlight on Mama's stone. She hadn't felt this calm in a very long time. Lydia closed her eyes and smiled, as the autumn wind pressed against her. She swore the scent of roses mingled with it. *You did this, Mama.*

"Hey, you there! You Fanny's girl?"

Lydia's eyes flew open. In the vicinity of her aunts' and uncle's graves, stood an elderly black couple. The old woman had her arm through the man's bent arm. Both of their heads were covered with wavy, white hair. Their clothes were drab, but neat.

"Cat got yer tongue, gal?" the old man asked.

"Huh? What?" Lydia swallowed hard. Where had they come from? She didn't recall seeing anyone, when she turned into the cemetery, but her mind had been on other things too.

"Well, gal, what's gonna be? You Fanny's gal or ain't cha?" the old man was quite persistent.

"Uh, if you mean, *Frances*, then yes, yes, I am." Lydia knew her voice shook.

"Oh, I see, if I mean *Frances*, then yes, you are!" the old man mocked her, and it scared her. He suddenly began to laugh. The old woman just stared at Lydia, and showed no emotion.

"I-I'm sorry, but do I know you?" They didn't seem familiar to her, yet they did. Even if they were old, you couldn't be too careful.

The couple began to take steps toward her. Why were they imposing on her time?

"We ain't imposin' nothin' on you!" the old man shouted.

"What? I never said—"

"You youngsters! All you think of is yer own time!"

"Sir, I beg your pardon, but this is my mother's headstone, and I intended to pay my respects." Lydia's anger began to build. "I'm getting married in a few hours, and I wanted my mother to be a part of it." Perhaps, by telling them the truth, they would leave her be.

"Oh, oh, so you is Fanny's gal!" The man and woman now stood on the opposite side of her mother's headstone. "Yup, now I can tell, you do favor Fanny, don't she, Ma?"

Lydia watched the old woman nod, but her eyes never left Lydia's face. "You know my mother?"

"Did I know yer mama?" the old man asked, who abruptly threw his head back again and laughed harder. "Don't ya recognize me, Tom—hey, what goes on there?" he couldn't finish his sentence since the old woman punched her bony elbow into the man's side.

Lydia couldn't mask her confusion. Who are these people?

He cleared his throat. "Yes, yea, I knew your mama. Daddy too. We all fished alot."

"You did? Hmm. Sorry, I don't remember you." Lydia ran her hands through her hair, but remembered Lacy still had to do some touch ups. She didn't want to ruin her hair anymore than she had.

"Oh, uh, well, you were a baby then. But there was this time, we were all over at Adel—" The old man stopped because the old woman elbowed him again.

"Look, I don't mean to be rude, but—"

"Oh, say here Ma, Little Miss Tom Cat don't wanna be rude. Hee, hee. She musta learnt her some manners, up there in the big city."

Lydia shook her head in frustration. "Please, I just wanted to spend some time with my mother before I head to the church." Why didn't they just leave? Lydia, without warning, felt uncomfortable.

"Your mother loved you more than life itself."

Lydia'a mouth dropped because these were the first words the old woman uttered.

The old woman continued, "Do you realize she did everything for you?"

"What?" Lydia was thoroughly confused "How do you know?"

The old woman heaved a sigh. Lydia feared it took all the woman's power to take a breath. "Your mama was pregnant with you, and the doctor told her to fear the worse. Either you'd be born dead or if you did live, there could be somethin' wrong with you, maybe even retarded."

"My God! How in heaven's name do you know *that*?" Instead of shaking her head in frustration, Lydia shook it in disbelief.

The old woman ignored Lydia and went on. "She pushed you, because she wanted you to be the best you could be. Fanny messed up along the way, sure. She didn't follow her own dreams. She wanted her dreams to be *your* dreams. Fanny had a difficult time excepting that you were your own girl."

Lydia was speechless and knew her eyes were the saucer size. Hadn't she just heard this, hours ago, when the moon was high? Lydia managed only to swallow. Getting to the church on time was no longer top priority.

"That blasted surgery Fanny decided she had to have! That was the beginning of the end. That surgery was the one thing she ever really did for herself. It turned out to be her most biggest mistake."

"But, how do you—"

"Her life, Lydia, she lived it for you. Do you know that? That surgery was Fanny's way of thinking she could live more for you. She wanted you to be proud of her."

"But I was proud of her! How could she think otherwise?"

"Were you Lydia, were you really?" the old woman's eyes became slits, while the old man remained silent.

"I didn't care about that! Mama was beautiful! When she had her hair fixed nice and her face was made up, I was worried I would *never* match up."

"Did you ever tell her that, Lydia?"

"I don't know!" *Why are you punishing me? Why are you picking a fight with me—at Mama's resting place, no less?* "I think I did. Geesh, I was just a kid."

"Maybe you were a child then, but parents need reinforcement too, no matter the age of the child. Not everything could center around you, Lydia. Your mother praised you, she needed some of the same. You let her down."

"I-I-"

"Lydia, what about *your* life? Have you come to terms after all these years?" the old woman's voice rose.

Lydia was certain the old man would crumble if the old woman gave way. "Ma'am, in all due respect to you, I'm not sure where you—"

"Where I what? Gal, I'm just asking you one simple question! Now, what you learned throughout this life? Life has changed for you overnight, hasn't it? Tell us how." the old woman's voice softened, yet her eyes continued to pierce through Lydia.

"Well, I really—"

"Gal, speak up!" the old woman demanded. "What have you taken in?"

Lydia gulped and her body trembled. Was she really forty or thirteen? She must say something. This old, creaky woman, wanted some kind of response. Lydia licked her lips. "Okay, all right. I was so young when she died. I just felt alone."

"But, Lydia, you were never alone." This time the old man spoke.

Lydia gazed into the old man's eyes. His were much kinder than the woman's. They were warm and familiar.

"Now, looking back, both of my parents loved me, more than I ever knew. Mistakes were made, on all of our parts. Me as an adolescent, then as an adult. Basically, I took Daddy for granted." Lydia sighed and looked down at the top of her mother's headstone, then caressed it. "Not until I was much older, did I fully comprehend what he endured. The torment, the not knowing, of how we both were going to turn out. I expected him to just take care of me. That was wrong. Just wrong. Daddy had so much strength. How did he do all of that? How did he keep sane for me?" Lydia brushed her tears away.

"He loved you, baby, that's how. He didn't want to lose you. People pushed him every which way when it came to you. He tried his best to be strong." the old woman said. "Dee had his lapses with alcohol and he lost faith a time or two. But when he saw you, he saw Fanny. He knew he couldn't let you down. He would rather die, than disappoint you."

Lydia looked past the couple, and up into the clouds of October. "Then me, my God—last night! I was with, no I dreamt, I was with Mama. We were together, just like when I was a little girl. She was just as pretty as I remembered." Lydia shut her eyes. The sun washed her face, as she tried to recall the memory. "I was so happy to see her, but then I went so berserk! I was so horrible to her!"

"How could *you* be so horrible?" the old man asked.

Lydia opened her eyes and feigned a smile. "I was, trust me! I yelled and screamed at her, not once, but twice! The second time, I, my goodness, I can't believe that I slapped her. I slapped my own mother!"

"What on earth for, Lydia? What possessed you?" The old woman asked. Her eyes had yet to soften.

Lydia nervously licked her lips. "Because I was so mad at her! She left me when I was thirteen. Thirteen! What could I know at that age? Mothers aren't suppose to die when they're children are kids. We're suppose to grow up together—be best friends. It did not happen. She made *sure* it didn't happen. My anger built for so very long. I didn't know what else to do. I loved her, but hated her all at the same time." Lydia bowed her head in shame. This was too much. Shouldn't she be at the church, getting ready for her wedding?

"And now?" the old woman's voice stung Lydia's ears.

Lydia raised her eyes to the still cold, slit eyes of the woman. "I realized I was acting out my childhood notions. I was thirteen years old again and being nothing less than a spoiled, whiny brat. I wanted my own way. I was so wrong. My mother gave me all she could in those short years we had. She tried to teach me what she could, and yes, mistakes were made. But even with those, the love never died."

"Seem like she might a learnt her way, afterall, Ma!"

"Hmm, have you Lydia?" the old woman asked. "Have you accepted things as they are?"

"I-I think so. I cannot deny I want her here to experience my wedding day. But I know she is in my heart. My parents sacrificed alot for me and I took it all for granted. I was wrong. I have been truly blessed to have Daddy all my life, Jewel for as long as I've had, and Mama for what I did have. I've always been surrounded by love. Some people never taste what I may have only considered an appetizer. I know that now. I've had a good life, and now with Seth, I begin a new chapter. My mother took the biggest risk, by wanting to give me life. How can I be angry with a woman that did that?" Lydia permitted a smile to cross her face.

She looked at the couple, and was surprised that both the old woman and the man had smiles as big as her own The old woman's eyes had finally melted.

"Well, gal," the old man started, "You better high tail it to the church. You got yourself a wedding to attend to!"

He was right! She'd lost all track of time. "Okay, you're right. I do need to go!" Lydia again, caressed the headstone's uneven top. "Since you know both my parents, please come to the wedding. It's at the First Christian Church on Lucinda. At seven o'clock. Please come!"

The old woman placed her hand over Lydia's and squeezed. Lydia was surprised that the woman's touch was warm. "Well, we'll try to make it, baby. But if we don't have a chance to see you, please be proud in knowing you are your mother's daughter. She is, and always will be proud of you." the old woman's voice was barely above a whisper. "Now, baby, put these flowers down on your mother's grave." the old woman handed Lydia six roses, three red and three yellow.

"Where did you—oh, never mind." She was now use to unexplained instances. "Thank you so much." Lydia balanced on her knees and placed them on her mother's grave. She fanned them, alternating the colors. "Mama loved roses. We had both colors of rose bushes in our yard. In the Spring, the scent would drift into my room, and—" When Lydia raised her head to look at the couple, there was only the October sky. *Why am I not surprised?*

Lydia ran her fingers over the letters that spelled out her mother's name. "This is a great day, Mama. You *are* here with me. Thank you so very much for this life. I love you." Lydia pressed her fingers to her lips, kissed them and then pressed those fingers to her mother's name. "Always."

•◆•

Getting dressed was a whirlwind. Lydia's attendants, friends from every part of her life, put in their two cents worth of stories and memories. Her hair, thankfully, wasn't as flat as she originally thought. Lacy didn't have to work any major miracle.

"Oh, look at her! She's not half bad! Far from those green knit pants and yellow and black tennis shoes, huh?" chirped Tilda.

"Hey, at least I was better lookin' than you wearin' your dad's bowling shirts! And with purple jeans yet!

"Or how 'bout the time we went to a Hawkeye game, and in a crowd of sixty thousand of our closest and dearest friends, Lyd's the only one to get caught with beer!" giggled Tess.

"Hey, remember when Lydia went through that 'I want to wear every color of mascara there is!' phase? And she wore black, gold, orange stuff , and even neon blue!" added Jane.

"Yea, that blue was so bright, one of my co-workers asked which electrical outlet she was plugged into!" piped Jeannie.

"And she's gotten worse, because now the size of her make-up case rivals the largest Samsonite suitcase ever made!" chimed Loree.

Everyone howled at Loree's deduction. The thing was, Lydia knew Loree was close to being on the money! "Ok, ok, you guys got me. But my make-up case not that big! I just brought my over night bag, for all the provisions I need!"

"Yea, babe, the only thing missing, in that thing, is your queen size bed! That comes *after* the wedding!" added Morgan.

"Hmm, so this is what friends are for, huh? Oh, well, I must say, though, I do look good, don't I?" Lydia loved using her vain tone around her friends. "Hey, how much time do we have? Has anybody seen Seth ? My luck, Mama Delaney locked him in his room!"

Another round of laughter ensued. Everyone was aware of the tussle between Lydia and her future mother-in-law. Starr eased her mind by informing her Seth was in his dressing room. He looked shaky, but was still breathing.

"Twenty minutes to go. And this Miss will be a Missus!" announced Tilda. "We should clear out of here and get into our places. The photographer has snapped her shots, so let's give the bride some moments to contemplate whether or not she's going to hit the road or stay in place!"

Lydia giggled. They knew her too well. 'Yes, I think I need some 'me' time!" Lydia hugged each of her friends as they filed from the room. Only Jewel and cousin Starr remained.

Lydia stepped in front of the mirror. This dress was absolutely divine! Seth will love it. *She* loved it. Sequins caught the room's light and shimmered in all their glory. Lydia barely believed she was looking at herself. Butterflies fluttered and flapped in her tummy again. She needed to get grounded and quick.

"Jewel, how did TZ get the cooler in my car? Did he come by the house this morning and put you and Daddy up to the joke?"

Jewel dabbed her eyes, as she looked at Lydia. "Oh, honey, no. Just like when TZ called this afternoon, he just said don't forget to get it back to him before you left town. Daddy and I had nothing to do with it." Jewel hands squeezed Lydia's arms. "You are so beautiful today! Starr, don't you think your cousin looks exactly like her mother right now?"

"Yes, she sure does! The kid doesn't look half bad, all dolled up. But afterall, it's in the genes!" chuckled Starr.

"What did you say, Starr?" Lydia sensed an air of deja vu.

"Oh, baby, Starr agrees that you look like your mother! So pretty! She would be so proud! I know I am!"

Someone knocked on the door. "Come in." Lydia mumbled.

"It's me, baby! You about ready?"

"Daddy, yes, come on in." Lydia dabbed her tears. She silently thanked the makers of waterproof mascara. Daddy looked spiffy in his dark blue suit. Hardly noticeable was the limp from his fake foot. He looked younger than his seventy some years. He looked good and smelled good—

"Oh no!"

"Lydia, what is it?" Jewel asked.

"I forgot some cologne! Daddy smelled so good, it triggered my mind!"

"You mean, in that horse's feedbag, you forgot something?" joked Dee. "You even came back into the house for pop!"

"I can't believe this! I must of left it in the bedroom. There's not enough time to go home and get it either! Do you have any, Jewel? Starr?" Lydia's heart sank as both women shook their heads. Lydia continued thumbing through her make-up bag, thinking she absent mindedly placed it in a different compartment. "Now what am I going to do? I bought that cologne especially for today! Ugh! Maybe one of the other girls has some."

"We still have a few minutes, honey, Starr and I'll go ask!" Jewel reached for the doorknob. "Come on, Starr, your legs are younger than mine! Now, Lydia, baby, you just stay put—and Dee, try to keep her calm." Jewel and Starr flew from room, women on a mission.

Dee fixed his eyes upon Lydia. She saw the pride and love shining from them. "We both get cleaned up pretty good, don't we, Father?'

"I'll say. We need to be on one of them fancy magazine covers!" Father and daughter shared a laugh. Then silence surrounded them. Dee returned his gaze to his daughter.

"Jewel said I look like mom." Lydia whispered. "Do you think so?"

"You look exactly like your mother. Sweety, you're my prettiest girl."

Daddy always said that to her. Even at the dawn of forty, Lydia was reduced to that five year old learning the way to Webster School. "I love you, daddy."

"And daddy loves you." Dee gently hugged her. "Now we need to get ready for this weddin'. Better take a look at that face. We don't want Mary Kay to run over you with a big ol' pink caddie, do we?" He always put a situation back on sound footing. "Hey, Lyd, I thought you didn't have any perfume?"

"Huh? I don't. I forgot it, remember?"

"Well, then what's this?" Dee had sauntered to a table where Lydia had spread her make-up. He held a small bottle of clear, brown liquid. "I'll be damned!"

"Daddy, what's the matter?' Lydia turned in his direction.

"I-I haven't seen this in years!" He murmured. "Where on earth did you get this? I didn't even think they made this stuff anymore."

"What stuff? Daddy, what are you talking about? Let me see that?" Lydia reached for the bottle. She noticed his eyes watered more than her own. "Oh my God! How could this be?"

"Lyd, this was your mom's favorite cologne. She loved this more than any other. The way it was packaged always made her laugh. And you were able to find some! More than twenty years later! How wonderful!"

Lydia was hypnotized by the petite gold letters on the bottle. They spelled: Straw Hat. She hadn't brought this! How did it get here?

"Baby, we got a few minutes, I'm gonna try to catch Jewel before she runs everyone ragged. Be back for you in a few. Make sure you put some of that good smellin' stuff on! Love you, baby." With a swift kiss on the cheek, Dee left her alone. The breeze from the closing door helped Lydia regain her senses.

Lydia stared at the bottle. She hadn't brought this! Daddy was right. This cologne hadn't been on the market for years. Where had it come from?

She unscrewed the bottle's top. The floral scent danced with her memories. The fragrance, light, and airy, smelled like the first new days of Summer. And yes, Mama had laughed at the packaging. *We talked about that last night, didn't we?*

Lydia placed her index finger on the top and tipped it. She dotted her neck, then behind her ears, and a dab behind the knees. The sensation made her smile. But how had it gotten here? Maybe a present from one of the girls?

"Don't forget your wrists."

Lydia spun around. Her gown made a swoshing sound as she faced the voice's direction. Lydia grabbed the table ledge for support. As she steadied herself, the truth stared her in the face.

•◆•

"You—" Lydia began as she stepped toward the person, who now stood with her.

"I'm here for a wedding."

"It really wasn't a dream, was it? We were together, weren't we? In that very short amount of time, right? I mean, Daddy said he turned off my light—"

"Yes, it all happened. God has a way of doing things. He can be pretty bossy like that!"

Both women grinned. "And He's probably the only boss you've ever listened to, huh, Mama?" Lydia teased.

"Well, something like that. Let's just leave it at that! Say, I was 'mother' toward the end of last night. What happened?" Frances shifted closer to her daughter.

"Well, I guess that was the grown-up side, but you'll always be Mama? Is that ok?"

"My angel, you are truly spectacular this day. Beautiful, does not express enough. I am so proud of you!" Frances squeezed Lydia's satin covered arms.

Lydia beamed and inspected her mother, who was not dressed in a robe. Instead, she wore a jacket and skirt suit, that were of the same golden white as her robe had been. Her hair was swept up in a chignon. "*You* are the one that is beautiful, Mama."

"Thank you, my angel. I wanted to look my best. Oh, and did you like my gift?"

"The Straw Hat? You did that?"

"As I recall, you needed something old. And that was my gift to you!

"No, Mama, your gift was being here with me. Nothing else rivals that! I am truly blessed! You, Daddy, Jewel, Starr, and my friends are with me today! I realized that more and more as the today wore on." Lydia firmly held her mother's hands. Soft, silky, and warm. Lydia searched her mother's eyes and smiled.

Lydia's revelation rang loud. When this adventure commenced, Lydia regarded Frances as if she were still a young girl. This was her mommy. The tide ebbed during the night and Lydia understood her review was far different now. They had connected as two women. She was no longer the teenager stomping her feet to get her own way. What she said to that elderly couple, was absolute truth.

"And don't forget us!" Behind Frances stood Mary, Grace, along with Uncle Hippy. They were dressed in robes, the same brilliant white as her mother's suit.

"Oh my goodness! I c-can't believe this!" Lydia threw her arms around each of them. They were as vibrant as she remembered.

"We couldn't miss this! You're our nifty niece!" stated Mary.

Lydia had to laugh, for 'nifty niece' was the title she crowned herself, when talking to either of them.

"I love this! You're all here! Grace and Mary, I've missed watching the stories with you! And Hippy, our times on the riverbank—Wait! Oh my gosh! Fishing—Hippy! Oh my! That was you, wasn't it? At Violet Hill earlier!" Lydia stood stunned. She waited anxiously for her uncle to answer.

"Tom Cat, we're never far!" Hippy informed her. "We look out for our niece. Always."

"Oh, no, I mean, oh yes! That was you! I was so flustered. But you, you called me Tom Cat! You did, didn't you? That was you! A—and at Fareway? I bet that was you too! I thought there was something familiar about you at the cemetery!"

Lydia watched her uncle look down, smile and show his dimples. They still gave him away. "Yes, Tommy it was me. She kept elbowing me, to shut me up. I 'bout blew it!"

"Hippy, why didn't you say something? And who was that woman? Was it either one of you? Mary? Grace?"

Both women shook their heads.

"Then who was—"

"Now, Lydia you have a wedding ceremony in a few minutes." Frances said.

"We are always near by, especially during my stories." Grace said.

"And I'm still waiting for you to make biscuits, even close to being, as good as mine!" added Mary.

"All right, the music is nearing the end. It's almost time." Frances announced.

Mama was right. The last bars of 'Moon River' soared through the church. The song would be repeated, then it was showtime. Butterflies flapped their wings faster. Lydia shut her eyes. She had to calm herself.

When she opened her eyes, only her mother stood before her. "I—hey, where did they go? That was quick. *Too* quick. Why did they leave? We needed more time."

"There is no time. You have a walk to make. People, and especially Seth Jacob Delaney are waiting and his mama, with her smelling salts!"

"Ha! That is the truth." Lydia smiled, then grew serious again. "But last night, Mama, time stopped. Why not now?"

"This is different, Lydia. Another time."

"Another time? You said that last night, too. And that means what?"

Before Frances could answer, a knock wrapped on the door.

"Baby, it's time."

"It's Daddy!" Lydia panicked. "You're here! What if he sees you?"

"Honey, it's fine. Open the door. It's time for him to do his fatherly duty."

"You're sure? What about all your light?

"Trust me. All is fine."

"Baby, you ok? Let me in. It's time."

Lydia swung the door open. "Sorry, Daddy, just trying to pull myself together. Everybody ready?"

"Yea, Jewel is already crying. She's wailin' so loud, she's gonna drown out the preacher! So talk loud!"

"I'm not surprised!" Lydia giggled as she reached for her bouquet of red roses. "Say, can you smell the Straw Hat, Daddy?"

"Mmm, I sure can! Just like Frances! I'd forgotten how good it smelled. Your mother always said it reminded her of the first days of Summer!"

"Really? That's what I think too!" *If only you knew, Daddy*!

Lydia made her way to the mirror. She decided she had to have one last go over. "How does everything look, Daddy?"

"Baby, you are perfect!"

"Hmm, I think you're biased!"

"That's what daddies are suppose to think! And you are my prettiest girl!"

Tears formed as Lydia smiled at their reflection. Daddy stood proud behind her. His hands gently held her arms. Her bouquet of red roses accentuated the picture splendidly. Lydia's smile broadened as she saw him wink at her. Then Lydia blinked. *Who is that in the mirror?*

A woman now stood to Lydia's left, in the space between her and Daddy. Lydia studied the woman. Things were similar, yet different.

This woman wore the same suit as Mama had. Her hair, also swept up and pulled back, just like Mama's. Only this woman's hair streaked of gray and her skin, even though etched slightly with wrinkles, glowed, just like Mama's!

This woman was obviously older than Mama. Yet, Lydia *knew*. Lydia reveled in the portrait before her. This solidified how their family would look, on this day of days, if Mama had lived. This older woman was Mama!

This was a seventy year old Frances Marie Burscot! The very age, Mama would be, if she were still alive. *This is truly my greatest gift.* For her family, in this moment in time, was now complete.

But didn't Daddy see her? All of a sudden, Lydia felt her mother's hand on her waist. The touch was gentle and warm, equal to the sensations from last night. Then Lydia watched in astonishment, as Frances placed her other hand under her father's!

Daddy can you feel it?

The organist sounded her cue. "Ok, girl, it's time" Dee ordered. "We have us a walk to take. And, no apples till its over!" Dee stepped away from the mirror and opened the door. "Say, did it get warm in here just now? Must be my nerves. You ready baby?"

"Warm? You feeling okay, Daddy?"

"Yea, just a kinda warm feeling all over my back. Haven't had a feeling like that since, well last night, but before—uh, feels okay now."

Dee extended his bent arm to Lydia and she took it without hesitation. She was ready to explode. Mama reached out and Daddy felt it, and evidently, may have, in the past. Mama really never did leave them. She had always been there.

Lydia glanced over her shoulder to see if her mother still remained. The seventy year old Frances waved and smiled back. A white handkerchief dabbed her eyes.

Lydia let Dee guide her from the dressing room. Time slipped away and Lydia knew she had to say something! It must not end like this! "I love you, Mama!"

"You say something honey?" Dee asked.

"Oh, just a silent prayer, Daddy!" Lydia said as she again glanced over her shoulder.

The door was closing on its own power. It closed on her mother. It closed on Mama. Their eyes met as the door inched farther.

Was this the final time? No, Mama said there might be another time. There just had to be! How could Lydia ever explain what had happened to her in the last twenty four hours? There was no way she could. Simple enough.

Lydia couldn't bare to watch the door close on her mother's face. Lydia straightened and faced the hallway before her. She inhaled deeply. This was it.

"Lydia. Lydia AnMarie Burscot turn to me!" The command came from behind her.

Lydia glanced at her beaming father. His attention was on the walk to the chapel. Once again, Lydia cocked her head over her shoulder. The door, realistically, should have shut itself by now. Yet, it stood ajar. Mama had not moved. Their eyes met.

"Remember, my darling angel, Mama love. Always." Frances pressed her fingers to her lips and blew a kiss. With that, the door shut firmly.

As the melody of the 'Wedding March' swirled about the chapel, euphoria replaced blood in Lydia's veins. She had been the recipient of a miracle. A *true* miracle!

On this day of vows, Lydia pledged another. From this day forward, because of this precious gift God had blessed her with, Lydia pledged her life's path would always prove most worthy of this gift. This was her choice and only hers! Amen.

· ◆ ·

After Frances told her angel she loved her and after the door closed, Frances stood alone. Head bowed. The scent of her daughter's bouquet of roses danced with her memories. Memories were now her only companion. Her only child now journeyed down the aisle of matrimony. God blessed her the gift to witness it.

For now, Frances prayed, her baby's questions had been answered. That now, for the first time in a long time, Lydia sensed peace and closure. Oh, there remained so much more.

Perhaps, during another day, she would tell Lydia that the woman, in the cemetery, was her maternal grandmother. A lady who died only a year after Lydia was born and cradled her every day since. Lydia would enjoy knowing that.

Another day might bring them together again. To talk and hopefully laugh. To cry, but always to love. Just the two of them. As only a mother and daughter could. As only two women can. Frances smiled at the prospect.

Before departing for her spot in the chapel, Frances pulled something from her suit's pocket. It was a photograph of Lydia, Dee, and herself, standing together. Frances traced their outlines with a finger. She smiled and then reached for Lydia's make-up case.

She chuckled, for Dee was right—it was as big as a horse's feedbag! She was confident Lydia could forget everything else in the entire world, but not this bag! She was her mother's daughter after all!

This photograph must not get lost, Frances reasoned. No, not this one. The bag's most secure spot, Frances decided, was beside the blue pointe shoes. The shoes would anchor the photograph down. The shoes were the 'something blue' Lydia's aunts and uncle left for her. Oh, how she would love them! Her baby would no longer be denied and finally, be on her toes!.

Frances heaved a contented sigh, for she was confident Lydia would cherish this photograph for all time. It wasn't a photograph from decades ago-when Lydia learned how to skate or ride her first two wheeler. No-this photograph was from only a moment ago, when the three of them stood together, as only they could. As a family-on this, her daughter's wedding day.

•◆•

About the Author

Lisa-Lin Burke, as like Lydia, lost her mother when she was thirteen. As millions of other daughters, she wondered how life could have been. With STRAW HAT, her first novel, Ms. Burke chose to explore emotions of growing up and coping with such a loss. Currently working on her second novel, the author lives in Dallas, Texas with her two Siamese cats, Brenner and Sammy.